RISE OF THE DRAGON KING

BOOK FOUR OF THE REALM SEERIES

LISA MANIFOLD

Rise of the Dragon King:
Book Four of The Realm Series

lisa@lisamanifold.com

OCEAN TOP PRESS

Created with Vellum

To Jimmy
Who has conquered his own Dragon Realm.

AUTHOR'S NOTE

This story is the fourth and final book of the Realm series. In between the novels, there are short stories, part of The Companion Stories, which are stories that detail brief snapshots of things happening in the Realms. You can find them in single book form, as well as part of THE COMPANION TALES VOLUMES ONE & TWO. The first four short stories are available as single stories as well as in THE COMPANION TALES VOLUME ONE. The last four stories and VOLUME TWO will be out later in the summer. While it's not necessary to read all The Companion Stories, it gives a richer look at the characters of the Realm. A complete list of the short stories are on my website. www.lisamanifold.com

I also want to thank all the readers who asked me,

after I gave Drake a failed love affair, what was going to happen to him outside of being Brennan's right-hand guy. Drake has become just as important to me as Brennan and Iris. I hope this answers the questions!

Enjoy!

Lisa

1

DRAKE

*D*rake rubbed his hands through his hair, trying to relieve the pressure he'd been feeling all day. It had been a long day. Nothing worked in this Realm – nothing. He couldn't figure out how Eilor had managed. The Castle was still standing. How he didn't know.

He thanked whatever luck he had that Brennan had allowed him to bring Taranath. Taranath was the Court Mage of the Goblin Realm, so his being here in the Dragon Realm wouldn't be permanent. The day Taranath had to go home was a day that Drake was dreading. While there were mages here – there were more mages than anything else – Taranath hadn't identified any of them that would be a good choice for the Court Mage. And since he was going to be the king of the Dragon Realm, he needed a mage.

Taranath remained positive that one would appear. He'd said so earlier today when Drake had checked in with him. Drake felt that he had shown masterful restraint and not inquired when one might fall from the sky. It was a good thing that Taranath could be so positive. Drake wasn't sure he could maintain the level of positivity that Taranath did. A trip down to the kitchens alone would cure that.

He scrubbed his face with his hands. Since he'd come to the Dragon Realm, he hadn't slept much. Too many things that commanded his attention wouldn't let him rest even when the day was done. *This* was why he'd never wanted to be a king. This was the sort of thing that would drive him mad or kill him.

At this point, Drake wasn't sure which would be better.

His attention shifted to the side table as the mirror from his father – the replacement mirror, he thought, thinking on the one Iris had forced him to leave with the shifter in the Human Realm – winked. Drake turned it over to see his father peering into the mirror.

"Drake?"

"I'm here, Father."

"I can't see a thing," Jharak sounded irritated.

"That's because I was trying to sleep."

"Did I wake you?" Jharak asked.

Drake noted that he didn't sound a bit sorry about it. "No, I'm lying here worrying over what I need to do next," he admitted.

Jharak laughed. "Welcome to leading a Realm, my son."

"There was a reason you called for me?" Drake didn't need his father giving him a hard time.

"Yes. I need you to join me. I have found Eilor," Jharak's mild tone belied the levity of what he was saying,

"What? Where?" Drake sat up, no longer tired. They'd been looking for Eilor since Cian and Ailla had attempted to take over the Fae Realm.

Had it not been for the efforts of his family—Iris, Brennan, Jharak, Taranath, and even Aine, he admitted —he wasn't sure that Cian and Ailla could have been defeated. Cian, in particular, had been extremely strong magically and driven by anger and lust for vengeance. Both were powerful forces and powerful motivators.

But they had prevailed. Cian was killed by Taranath, and Ailla by Dhysara. Dhysara, the daughter of the Goblin King before Brennan, had fled to the Dragon Realm with her mother when the old Goblin

King had died. Eilor took them in and nurtured the sense of being wronged. That was also where Dhysara met Cian. Cian, known to the Dragon Court as Kelan, had been the eldest son of the Fae King, who was thought to be dead. Another fugitive hidden away by Eilor.

Drake felt sorry for Dhysara. But she didn't desire the pity of anyone. She'd known Cian as Kelan and had chosen to remember him as Kelan, nothing more. She'd made her choice to move on, and forget anything associated with Cian. Drake hoped that she would never remember.

Which brought him back to Eilor. Damn the man. Everything he touched, everything he did—it was tainted. Or felt tainted. Drake felt like he was part of scrubbing the filth away from the Realm.

Why had no one noticed this about Eilor before? How had the man gotten away with so much that was subversive? He wondered if that was due to Ailla.

Ailla. He pushed the thought of her away as Jharak continued to speak.

"I'm at the edge of the Fae Realm, where it borders both the Troll and the Goblin Realms," Jharak replied.

"I know where that it. Is Brennan with you?"

"He's on his way."

"It will take me some time," Drake said, thinking about how he'd need to set things in motion to be able to leave. He'd never before appreciated how a well-run Realm made all things easier. But it did. When the Realm existed in a constant state of disarray as was the case with the Dragon Realm, nothing was simple. Nothing went smoothly.

"Get here as soon as you can. I need to be able to provide witnesses that we did indeed find him, should there be questions." The mirror winked out.

No longer tired, Drake spoke to the mirror again. "Aine, Taranath."

He waited. Aine was the one who answered her mirror first.

"Yes?"

"Can you please come to my chambers? I have to leave for a time," he said.

She nodded, and the mirror went dark for only moments before he saw Taranath.

"My lord?"

"Can you please come to my chambers?" Drake asked. He knew he didn't have to give a lot of explanations to Taranath.

The mirror went dark, and Drake swung his legs out of bed, taking the mirror with him as he got dressed. He put on his leather armor, and belted his sword around his waist, making sure to tuck the mirror into a side pocket. Just as he finished, he heard the outer door to his chambers open. He left his sleeping room and went out to see who'd arrived.

It was both Aine and Taranath.

"Good, I'm glad you're here so quickly. Thank you," Drake said. Now that he'd agreed to be the king, he noticed that even those who knew him well gave him less discussion when he asked them to do something. Not that he'd say he knew Aine well. But she and Taranath were the only people he knew he could trust at this point.

"What's happened?" Aine asked. As always, she spoke quietly.

Drake knew that others found her restful. Iris had said as much before he'd left the Goblin Realm. He didn't. He always felt like he had an itch he couldn't quite reach when in her presence. It was worse when she took him down to see Fangorn and the other dragons. He guessed it was due to the massive amount of magic and everything else that went along with the dragons. He'd seen a lot in his time in the Fae and Goblin Realms since Jharak had adopted him, but nothing affected him like seeing the dragons.

And that was with only a handful of them. He couldn't imagine what it had been like where there had been an entire Realm of dragons.

"My father let me know that he's located Eilor," Drake said.

Aine's expression sharpened. "Where is he?"

Seeing her face, and taking a guess at her thoughts, given all he knew of what Eilor had done to her, Drake thought the former king had been fortunate to die before Aine found him. He'd been horrified when Aine had shared the some of the contents of Eilor's journals. She was fairly protective of them. Drake understood. It was one thing to know your history. That had been Aine's goal initially. Once she'd read them and shared with him her history, she'd surprised him by giving him the journals. For safekeeping, and she'd told him that he could read them if he wished.

He'd put them in his wardrobe and locked it shut. He didn't want to read them.

While he understood her desire to know, it was something else entirely to have your history laid open to others. He'd heard enough of the behind-the-hand comments about his human beginnings. He'd been adopted by Jharak and Nerida, the Fae King and Queen, when he was young, barely into double digits, age-wise. But six-hundred and sixty plus years later, he still heard the whispers of "human-born" when he visited the Fae Castle. One more reason that he'd preferred to spend time in the Goblin Realm. The goblins didn't care that he was human-born. He wasn't a goblin, which was how they divided the world. To goblins, all non-goblins were less than, and frankly, to be pitied. Goblins were remarkably happy with their place in the world.

He realized that he'd not yet answered Aine. "Apparently, he's dead."

Aine said, "Did Jharak kill him? Personally? Or see him die?"

"No. He found his body, or at least that is my understanding. We didn't speak long. He just called to order me to him, and that was it."

Aine pursed her lips. "I wouldn't be so sure, then."

Taranath spoke then. "The Lady Aine has a point. From what I can tell from working with his—"

"Stable of mages?" Drake asked.

"I wouldn't call them a stable, My lord, but it is a sizable group. As I was saying, from speaking and working with them, Eilor and Niles were both the skilled practitioners. These poor children were merely there to provide the bodily energy that Eilor required for his work. They know very little. It's extremely neglectful to gather so many with talent and then stifle them." Taranath sounded stern, which was unlike him.

"I am empathetic, Taranath, but what has that to do with whether or not the blasted man is dead?" Drake tried to keep a rein on his temper. All he wanted was to tell them how to handle things and get going.

After several weeks in the castle, he found that he

missed his life in the Goblin Realm. Well, not entirely, but he missed the simple pleasure of being able to do what he wished and to handle a problem directly. As even the supposed king, he didn't get that luxury any longer. There was always someone who would take care of things.

"Do you believe he would give up everything he had in motion?" Aine asked. "He put a great deal of work and time into his plans with the dragons, and I can't believe that he pinned all his hopes on Cian and Ailla." Her voice dropped into scorn as she said the name of the now deceased princess of the Dragon Realm.

Drake wondered if she even knew she did it. He didn't blame her. From the little she'd told him, and what he'd seen recently, Ailla was a horrible tyrant to be around. She'd been very cruel to Aine. Her bias aside, she made a good point.

"You may be right. But we have to go and see. That's why I asked you to join me. I need to go. I want to see this for myself, but I find myself worried about leaving. I must leave the Realm in your hands."

Taranath nodded. "You can trust us, My lord."

Drake knew that. It made leaving a little easier. In spite of his eagerness to be gone, he worried what would await him when he returned.

Aine scowled. He stifled a sigh. What now?

"I make no promises that I'll do as you would," she said.

That was the best he could hope for. Aine retained her love/hate relationship with the Realm. Once again, even though he didn't want to admit it, she was justified in her feelings.

But there was no time for that now.

"I will be happy with that, my lady," Drake said wryly, giving her a slight bow. "May I ask that you please consult with Taranath before taking some crazed action?"

Aine glared, and then the hint of a smile tipped the corner of her mouth. "Very well. I promise to allow the restraint of the mage to keep the Realm safe in your absence."

Drake laughed, relieving a tension he didn't know he'd been feeling. "We can all thank the stars for that," he said.

That made even Taranath smile.

"Will you contact me to let us know when you are returning, My lord?" Taranath asked. "The magic that I have seen hints of are not things that I have experienced before. If it is indeed Eilor, who knows what sort of magic he has about him, even after he has died."

"Worried, mage?" Drake teased.

"I am," Taranath said simply. "From an academic

point of view, this is fascinating. It's a bit more dangerous on a personal level," he finished.

Having met the dragons, and felt the sheer power that radiated from them even while they slept, Drake could believe it. They were connected to Realm somehow. If Taranath were unable to make the connection thus far, this was advanced magic.

"You are the master of the understatement, Taranath. But I trust you with everything here. Now I must go. I am surprised my father hasn't called with a ready scold for how long it's taken me."

"Shall I help with the portal?" Taranath asked.

"Since you're here," Drake said. He described the place. Taranath knew the Realms as well as any of the kings—a group which he, Drake, was almost a part of, he realized. He just didn't think of himself that way.

Taranath waved his hand. When had he begun to do this without a stone? When they'd gone to rescue Brennan, Taranath had used stones like everyone else. He made a mental note to ask the mage about it once he returned. One more thing on the list of things to handle.

But it would need to wait. One thing at a time. He waited for the portal to widen, and then stepped into the dark circle within the light of the portal. It was one of the reasons he hated to portal at night. You couldn't see what it was you were walking into. He drew his sword from the scabbard and stepped all the way through.

The heat from the different landscape was the first thing that hit him.

Then it was the edge of a very fine, very sharp blade.

"*Y*ou are?" A gruff voice inquired.

"I am Drake, son of Jharak." He let his voice ring out.

"The King of the Dragon Realm," Jharak's calm tones stopped any further discussion.

"My lord," said the gruff voice.

Drake could hear the apology in it. He was glad to know that Jharak hadn't come alone. He'd brought his King's Guards, who were committed to serving the Fae King. He wasn't sure how he felt with Jharak naming him so.

Then he frowned because he knew that his father couldn't see him. It was another manner of Jharak making sure that Drake walked the path he wanted. Drake didn't know why he still resisted so much. He'd agreed to take the throne. The time for the coronation was set. His Castle was in an uproar over it. But he couldn't help his mulish thoughts.

"Thank you, father," he said. The sarcasm was evident.

"You are welcome, your majesty," Jharak said cheerfully.

Whenever he forgot that his father had been leading not only his Realm but all the Realms for far longer than Drake had been alive, Jharak reminded him in small ways. Not that he thought Jharak did it consciously. But the man was a consummate leader, capable of handling all situations. The only time Drake could remember his father being slightly off balance was the recent confrontation with Cian.

Of course, since Cian was his son, it was understandable.

"Well? Where is the bastard?" Drake asked.

"This way," Jharak turned and waved to a general area in front of him.

"Can you tell how he died?"

"He was stabbed. Multiple times," Jharak said in a way that suggested he wasn't surprised.

"Do you believe it's him?" Drake asked.

"I know what he looks like, and it's him. He is also wearing the ring," Jharak said.

"What ring?" Drake had no idea what Jharak was talking about.

"After the dragon war, when the dragons conceded, they crafted a ring. It was part of the Realm, and their making it was an agreement that one of the fae would now lead the Dragon Realm. It was given to Eilor when he took the throne, and I have never seen him without it."

"Is it magic?" Drake wondered why he was only hearing this now. Then he thought about the truth behind the responsibilities of the Goblin King. Most fae felt the Goblin Realm was a punishment. Not a Realm that was considered desirable. That Brennan, the youngest of the two sons of Jharak, had been made the heir out of necessity. Nothing could be further from the truth. Only the most skilled of magical practitioners were called to the Goblin Throne. The job of the Goblin King was to keep the magic of the other Realms in balance. Such responsibility could not be entrusted to just anyone. That information only made it to those who needed to know. Perhaps this was a similar situation.

"It is, in that it binds the fae-born Dragon King to the Dragon Realm. The dragons who ruled were a part of the land," Jharak explained easily, as though he wasn't standing in a remote corner of his Realm in the dark. "They felt, and I agreed, that it was important for anyone who was the king of the Realm to be connected as they had been." Jharak tapped his chin, thinking. "I wonder if that was part of why we've ended up where we are."

"It might have been nice to know this before this moment," Drake said dryly, thinking of his conversation with Taranath before he'd left.

"If what was part of this?" Brennan came up behind them as they walked.

"Drake," he said, clapping Drake on the shoulder.

Drake smiled. He'd been away from the Goblin Realm long enough that he'd forgotten how right it felt to be with his brother. But things were different – even as he enjoyed being with his family, a part of his mind was back in his—the Dragon—Realm.

His Realm. He was going to be the king. He'd agreed to be the steward of this Realm, and now he was thinking of it as his. He supposed that was a good thing.

"The King's ring helped to tie a fae man to the Dragon Realm. I am considering that the ring may have made Eilor more ambitious than he was before," Jharak said.

Drake shook his head, even though he was sure the other two couldn't see him. "No. I disagree with that. I've seen parts of Eilor's journal. I believe he was always this ambitious. Becoming the king was merely an opportunity. Having read some of his thoughts, he would have found an opportunity no matter what." He stopped, not wanting to share information that he didn't feel was his to share.

"That's right, Aine found them, didn't she? Will you send them to me?" Jharak asked.

Drake surprised himself at the flare of protectiveness he felt for Aine at that moment. He knew the exposure—and the censure—she would face. He couldn't do that to her, even for his father. No one but the two of them knew her parentage at this point. He thought she'd probably tell Taranath, but not yet.

"I don't know, Father," he said as they continued walking. "While I understand why you want to see them, there is a lot that is particular to Aine, and I think it's up to her to decide what she shares."

"Have you read them?" Brennan asked.

"No. I've seen a bit, but for the most part, Aine has related to me the things she thinks I need to know." Drake couldn't explain why he didn't tell them that Aine had recently given him the journals for safe keeping. She'd mentioned that it made her sick to have them close. Given what she'd told him about all she'd learned, he could understand. And knowing that, he hadn't been able to read them. Not to mention he had no time or inclination for any more reading. He was swimming in parchment as it was.

A moment of silence followed his words. Jharak stopped, holding up his hand. "He's right down there. But I have to ask you, Drake, do you feel it wise to be receiving information piecemeal like that? While I respect Aine greatly, there is a difference in what you— we—might find important versus what she does."

Drake could feel the weight of his father and brother awaiting his answer. Annoying as she was, he couldn't betray Aine. He understood her.

"She wants the best for the Realm, Father, and I believe she wants the best for all of us. She's had an odd upbringing, to say the least. But I have seen how she talks to Iris, and to you, and Taranath—"

"How does she talk to you?" Brennan interrupted.

"With great restraint and a general feeling of being put upon," Drake shot back, grinning. "I seem to inspire that sort of response everywhere I go."

Another moment of silence greeted his words. He felt the itchy feeling that usually only came after spending a long time with Aine.

"Well, I respect your loyalty to her, as a citizen of the Dragon Realm," Jharak said.

Brennan made a noise that sounded very much like muffled laughter. Drake glanced at him, but couldn't see Brennan clearly in the dark.

"She's suffered a great deal under Eilor," Drake said, thinking on what he had heard. Seeing Aine's face in his mind's eye, and hearing the tone of her voice as she related what she'd read. He knew, without having to be told, that it was far worse than she shared. "She deserves that from us," he finished. He may as well make this a family obligation. If it weren't for Aine, there was no guarantee that he, Taranath, and Iris would have been able to rescue Brennan. *We do owe her,* he thought. *I'm going to make sure we do the right thing for her.*

Another silence. "I agree. You are doing the right thing," Brennan said.

"I'd like you to ask her to share what she can," Jharak said. "And to warn us of anything she feels might be harmful to all the Realms."

"Of course," Drake said. As if Aine would do any less.

He wondered what was wrong with him. He didn't give her this much of a benefit of the doubt when he had to deal with her on a daily basis.

Or perhaps he did.

He didn't want to think about it.

"Shall we go and look at the mad bastard before he starts to stink?" Drake asked, wanting to change the subject.

A guard approached them with a torch, and he caught a glimpse of his father's face. Jharak watched him with a slight smile. What was that for?

Then he noticed that Brennan had the same look on his face.

"What?" He asked, looking between the two of them.

"Nothing," Brennan said, looking at Jharak once more. "Nothing at all," he added as Jharak grinned. "You're right, Drake. Let's focus on dealing with the hopefully very dead Eilor." Brennan turned away without saying anything else.

Jharak smiled, watching Brennan. His eyes met Drake's. "Let me know what happens with Aine. I'm happy to hear whatever she wishes to share."

Drake knew that his father was disappointed, but it didn't show as Jharak followed Brennan.

What had they been talking about? Had he missed something? It felt as though ever since he'd come to the Dragon Realm, the entire world had tilted sideways.

Drake shook his head and made his way down the small hill where Brennan and Jharak stood over a bundle on the ground.

"Is this him?" He asked.

Drake saw that a guard was kneeling by the body, and at a nod from Jharak, he removed the cloak that someone draped over the head. A gesture of respect not deserved by the man on the ground, Drake thought. But then, he reminded himself, they were not inhumane, even to monsters.

"It's him," Brennan said grimly. "I don't know whether to be glad or disappointed that it is, but it's him."

"Does he have the ring?" Drake asked. He was curious to see the ring now.

Jharak knelt down, pulling a square of cloth from his pocket. He picked up Eilor's hands, first the left, and then the right. He pulled the right hand closer, forcing the body to turn towards him.

The sound of Eilor's various bits of clothing brushing against one another, brushing against the body of a dead man, made Drake's skin crawl. Given all the dead he'd seen in his life, this felt all wrong.

Something wasn't right.

3

DRAKE

"Be careful," Brennan said, looking over Jharak's shoulder.

Jharak didn't reply, but using the cloth, carefully removed a ring from Eilor's right hand. "Light," he said, not looking up.

Another guard came close, holding a torch. The man lifted it above Jharak, and then down so that it was possible to see the ring.

It was a massive gold ring, with three dragons chasing one another and a large blue stone set in the center of the three dragons. As Jharak turned it over, Drake could see that the tails of the dragons made up the shank and the rest of the ring.

Jharak turned it again, and an arc of flame shot from the ring. It went towards Jharak's face, and both

Drake and Brennan yelled at the same time. Jharak dropped the ring, throwing himself backward as he did so.

The ring and the cloth fell to the ground, and the guard leaned over with the torch, trying to keep the ring in sight.

"What was that?" Drake asked, stepping to Jharak to offer him his hand. He pulled his father up, looking him over to see if there was any outward injury.

"I'm fine," Jharak said, brushing himself off. "Annoyed, but fine. As to what it was, I don't know. Where's the ring?"

The guard gestured with the torch. It lay just outside the brightest circle of light. Drake found the cloth and stopped Jharak as he made for the ring once more.

"Let me. You're more valuable," Drake grinned. "And we can't let you touch it, lordship," he looked at Brennan. "I have enough problems without your wife at me for letting you get hurt. How did you get away on your own, by the way?" He stepped closer to the ring and positioned the cloth in his hand.

"I told her I had to. As well, Iris is not feeling as well as she would like. She assures me that this is normal. She is as anxious for this matter to be resolved as the rest of us," Brennan said. "Why would there be a problem?"

Drake met Jharak's eyes, and they both laughed. "Oh, I don't know. She hasn't let you out of her sight since you returned," Drake said. He didn't refer to the fact that Iris had been very worried Brennan would die, or that now she was pregnant and no one wanted to cross words with her.

To his surprise, Brennan just smiled. "A good wife is attentive," he said mildly, as though Drake weren't needling him covertly.

Drake let it be. While he liked to tease his brother, he was very happy for him. Iris made him extremely happy. Even though he hadn't cared for Iris much at the beginning, as he was sure she was a spy of some sort, he was very fond of her. She'd shown a great deal of strength and courage when they set out to rescue Brennan from Cian. And she had become very powerful magically. That only happened if one, particularly a human raised with no magic, spent a lot of time practicing. Drake respected courage and hard work. And Iris loved Brennan, which was the most important thing.

He reached down and picked up the ring, cradling it in his hand. He could feel nothing out of the ordinary, although he had the cloth protecting him.

"I want to see if this hurts both of us," Drake said, and he dumped the ring into his other, bare hand.

"No!" Shouted Brennan and Jharak as one. They

leaped towards Drake, who stretched his hand out in front of him, showing them it was unharmed.

"Nothing happened," he said.

"Why did it react to me and not to you?" Jharak frowned.

If this wasn't such a serious moment, Drake might have laughed. His father didn't often lack the answer.

"Perhaps it's because Drake is the Dragon King?" Brennan crossed his arms, looking at Drake critically.

"But he hasn't been crowned yet." The frown deepened between Jharak's eyes.

"Does that affect things?" Drake asked.

A moment, and then Jharak sighed. "I don't know. It's been so long since Eilor was crowned, you could tell me that he had to dance about with a crown of weeds on his head and I couldn't confirm or deny it. He's the only non-dragon ever to be crowned. I hate to do this to you since I know that you are trying to tread carefully," he looked at Drake. "But I need you to have Aine bring you back to Fangorn."

He held up a hand as Drake opened his mouth. "I know that you're not entirely comfortable with them. I know that they hate me, and with reason. But I am not a dragon, nor do I have the connection to that Realm that Fangorn does. Have Aine ask for an audience. Make it formal. Dragons love formality and respect. I do hope you've been so when you were there before."

"Did you ever have to be in the same place as one?" Drake asked.

Jharak nodded.

"Then you will remember that they feel overpowering, and it's pretty intimidating."

"Says the brave warrior," Brennan snickered.

"When you realize that the being in front of you can sizzle you to the consistency of burnt meat, you manage to find some respect," Drake shot back. "Speaking of being burnt to a crisp, how is Mother?"

Jharak exhaled in an exaggerated manner. "Your mother is fine. Not wonderful, not horrible. But fine."

Drake and Brennan looked at one another.

"Is she still not talking to you?" Brennan asked.

"She is very sad and very angry. It's going to take some time for her to heal," Jharak said in the tone of one who was repeating the same thing many times over.

"Is she still mad at all of us?" Drake asked. He forgot about the ring as he thought of his mother. How did one grieve a son that she thought lost so many years ago? Worse, how did one grieve for a son who did his utmost to kill you and the rest of your family?

That had been Cian's goal—to kill them all and rule over the Fae Realm, which meant all the Realms —with Ailla.

At the thought of Ailla, which Drake had

studiously been avoiding beyond a superficial level of consideration, he immediately felt empathy for his mother.

He would never admit it aloud, as he had trouble admitting it to even himself, but he had wept for her the night she died in front of him. Why he cried, he didn't know. Drake realized that she had never really loved him, not as he loved her. Not in any way that could be considered real.

But it had still pierced a small corner of his heart to see her die, even though he would have killed her himself if it had come to that. He recalled the conversation he'd had with Iris before they'd set out to find Brennan. He'd told her that he had already decided that Ailla had to die.

He hadn't been lying. Drake had, however, omitted how he felt about it. Secretly, he hoped that someone else would kill her. He had no problem killing Cian, but Ailla? He didn't want to be the one to do it.

As it was, he hadn't been the one who delivered the killing blow. Dhysara had knocked Ailla flat, taking the life from her. She'd done it without batting an eyelash. Drake was very glad that Dhysara had chosen to have her memory of anything about Cian and the night he died removed. She wanted to remember him as she knew him before his lust for vengeance and power changed him. Or rather, brought out the rotten man that Cian was at his core.

It had still hurt to see Ailla fall lifeless, an unanswered question on her lips. He missed her; the woman he'd fallen in love with. His rational mind knew that woman never existed, but that didn't seem to matter when it came to his heart.

"She takes the loss of Cian hard still," Jharak answered.

Drake started, yanked from his thoughts. "Well," he said, to cover up the fact that he'd been woolgathering, "She is going to need to put on a happy face. If I'm going to go through with this coronation nonsense, the Fae Queen will be there." His voice hardened. "She can mourn all she wants, and never speak to me in private until her mourning has passed, but she will present a united front to those outside this family."

Jharak raised his brows. "Are you willing—" then he stopped, and looked down at Drake's hand. "Where is the ring?"

"What?" Drake looked down.

"The cloth is there," Jharak pointed at a spot on the ground.

He hadn't realized that the cloth had dropped away. "The ring is in my hand," Drake said, opening his hand. It didn't hurt. He hoped that nothing would happen. Particularly as he didn't want to admit he'd been thinking about...Well, what—or rather, whom he'd been thinking about.

"Your hand is fine," Brennan said. "Bring the light over here, please," he said over his shoulder to one of the guards.

The man came over and held a torch over them. Jharak leaned over to see the ring.

"Why didn't it burn you?" He asked, turning Drake's hand over in his, careful not to touch the ring. Drake wondered if his father realized he'd asked this already.

"Because as I said, Drake is the Dragon King. It doesn't matter that he has not been officially named as such," Brennan said in the manner of one explaining something to a child. "He is working for the good of the Realm. If there is as much magic as we suspect, the Realm has accepted him."

When both Drake and Jharak looked at him in disbelief, Brennan shrugged. "It makes sense," he said. "I don't see why you're surprised. It's like the Goblin Realm. We haven't had more than one Dragon King, or I think we would have seen this before."

"It does make sense," Jharak said slowly, letting go of Drake's hand. He was looking at the hand that held the ring, but Drake could tell that he was deep in thought. Then he looked up, and it was clear he'd made a decision.

"Take the ring to Taranath. Have him study it before we have to use it in the coronation ceremony. See if one of the many mages that he says are hanging about the place have any idea what is going on with the ring. Even dead, the man is a menace," Jharak huffed.

"Do you think I might have my mage back sometime in the foreseeable future?" Brennan asked. "I realize we all serve at your pleasure, but he is the mage for the Goblin Realm."

"He is the best person for this," Jharak said. "If I didn't have such a fondness for you as my son, I would take Taranath for the Fae Court," he grinned at Brennan. "But since I love my sons, I choose to make the sacrifice."

Drake laughed at the eye roll Brennan threw their father.

"Good as this familial affection is, I fear if I leave the Dragon Realm on its own too long, something may go badly amiss," he admitted.

"Is it that bad?" Brennan asked.

"How the man managed to feed himself is a mystery. Nothing works smoothly, and there is no sense of community, or working together. If he wasn't dead," Drake nudged the body with his foot, "I might stab him myself."

Jharak laughed. "It's painful at the beginning, but

once you get things running smoothly, you'll forget how wretched this time was. You need to find a good steward."

"And a good mage," Brennan.

Drake sighed. "Taranath is convinced that one will appear. I don't see how myself, but his optimism is undimmed."

"It's one of his gifts," Brennan said. "I've learned not to doubt him."

"I hope he's right. I've seen all the would-be mages that worked with Eilor," Drake said. "They don't look old enough to be on their own, much less be the chief mage for a Realm."

"Have faith in Taranath," Brennan said. "He won't leave you with someone not up for the task. Will you send word once Taranath's had a chance to study the ring?"

Drake nodded. "He'll love it. The scholar in him is like a child. He's practically quivering with excitement to meet the dragons, but that hasn't happened yet."

"I'm glad that Fangorn is willing to talk with Aine regularly."

"He loves her," Drake said bluntly. "You can see it on him when he talks with her. She's part of his family, and he feels strongly about family."

"Which may create a problem, as the rest of the Realms are the reason he has no more family," Jharak said. "Well, we'll have to deal with that when it comes up. It can't be changed." He turned to a guard. "Get two men to carry the body home. We need to bury him discreetly."

"Will you let the rest of the Realms know?" Brennan asked.

"In due time," Jharak said.

"The coronation is soon," Drake pointed out.

"I will release the announcement in the appropriate time," Jharak said, exasperation showing in his tone. "I do have some experience in managing the affairs of the Fae Realm."

"Well, don't leave it too long, Father," Drake said. "And tell Mother that I expect to see her. With a smile."

That made Jharak grin. "Oh, I'll tell her. I wish you luck."

"I will be fine," Drake said. While he felt for his mother, he wasn't going to back down on this request. If he was going to take on the damn Realm, she could manage a few smiles and pleasantries.

"Well, with that settled, I'm off," Brennan said with a smile. "I don't want to worry Iris any more than she already is."

"You're hopeless, lordship," Drake said.

Brennan waved a hand and disappeared into the darkness. A moment later, a circle of light showed that he'd opened his portal. The portal brightened and then faded.

"I'll expect to hear from you when Taranath finishes his inspection," Jharak said. "Be well, my son." He clasped Drake on the shoulder, and then he too disappeared.

Drake watched as Jharak appeared again, directing the transport of Eilor's remains. He turned, and pulling a stone from his belt, opened a portal. It was time to go home.

4

AINE

I studied the ceiling above my head. I'd been lying here ever since Drake had called us to his rooms to announce that he was leaving. When he said he was leaving, my heart nearly came out of my chest. He couldn't. He couldn't leave.

When I'd met him, he bothered me. I had no reason for it. He just bothered me. Perhaps this is what having an annoying sibling was like? Ailla had often said I was the sad family secret no one wanted to be around. That was the only experience I had with anything resembling a sibling.

I'd been nine at the time Eilor introduced me to Cian. He'd looked fondly on the man, as though he were a smaller, favorite child to be indulged, and said that I could be a proper sibling for Cian.

One look at Cian told me that would never happen. He barely waited until Eilor had left the room to began harassing me. It didn't help that Niles, Eilor's pet mage, encouraged Cian in his cruelty to me. Why Niles, a grown man, would concern himself with me when I was just a child made no sense. I still didn't understand it, although my personal opinion was that Niles just hated me.

I'd finally understood why, when Ailla, in her normal bad mood, screamed at me one day. Cian and Ailla were close, in a way that excluded everyone else. She resented that her father had thought of throwing Cian and me together. And Cian knew that there was something different about me, something that Eilor wanted. That made me of value. Cian wanted to have me because Eilor did.

And it made Ailla crazy. It also made Niles crazy. In some strange manner, they saw me as competition for Eilor. The thought made me shudder. Why they wanted to be the focus of Eilor or Cian's attention was something sick I couldn't fathom. Catching the eye of either of them never turned out well for me.

As for Cian, it didn't matter that he didn't know what it was. But if someone else valued it, Cian wanted it. He was like a child, taking whatever he wished for, going into rages when he didn't get it. Whatever I was, if Eilor valued me, Cian wanted me. He never knew the real story of my past. Which infuriated him, and was why he was so cruel to me.

Niles knew. Which was why he let Cian do as he did.

As for Ailla, everyone knew he was officially promised to Dhysara, but everyone outside of Dhysara and her mother knew that Cian—or Kelan, as he was known then—loved Ailla. As much as he could love another, I supposed. My thought was that the only person Cian cared about was himself, although he put forth some effort for the two women he toyed with.

I thought about that moment when he died. He'd been genuine in his emotion over Dhysara being pregnant. It was the first time I'd seen that in him. He'd always seemed so calculating.

I didn't want to think about him anymore. He was dead, and horrid Ailla with him. I felt no pity at their passing. Had they succeeded in their plans, this world would be worse off. No one would be safe, and everyone would suffer.

And that was before the plots of Eilor came into it.

I couldn't think of him either. That led me to all I'd learned in his journals, and that made me want to break down like a child and weep and smash something to bits all at once.

The one fact that I kept coming back to was that I was not alone. I'd grown up believing that I had no family. Eilor's refusal to tell me anything about them made me think that they were horrible people. He'd hinted that he'd done me a favor by taking me in. Given how I was treated, why would I believe anything else? My family must have been wretched if Eilor was better.

I hadn't considered that he might be hiding something from me. That there was a reason that he chose not to tell me the truth. In looking, I wondered why. But I knew. I'd been convinced of my unworthiness. I didn't even question it. Until I'd found the journal documenting my family history, I was sure they were even worse than Eilor.

He'd robbed me of that, too. Along with anything resembling normalcy.

But now, things were different. I had people who cared for me. I didn't know if they were at the level of family, but there were people who cared. In spite of how Drake seemed to get under my skin, I trusted him. And I trusted Taranath. I also trusted Iris. Because of her, I was willing to trust Brennan. Jharak made me nervous. I didn't think he was a bad person, however. Eilor had constantly grumbled about how dismissive Jharak was towards him, so that made me inclined to think well of Jharak regardless.

And I had a brother. That brought up an entirely different set of feelings in me. While cleaning out the rooms that Eilor had lived in, I'd found three journals that detailed what Eilor had been up to for hundreds of years.

When Eilor had been given the Dragon Realm to lead, one of his responsibilities was the care of the few remaining dragons that were the last of their race alive after the dragon wars. I hadn't been alive, obviously, but apparently, the dragons had tried to take over all the Realms and waged a pretty major war. Jharak had been the Fae King at that time, and with the other Realms, had defeated the dragons. From the conversation I'd heard, it was not an easy victory. All the dragons had died, except the dragons that lived below the Dragon Castle.

Before Eilor's death, I'd been down to see the dragons with him. In particular, he wanted me to meet Fangorn. At the time, I hadn't understood why. After reading the journals I'd found, I understood. It thrilled me and made me sick.

Fangorn, the dragon fae shifter, was my grandfather. Eilor had brought countless women to Fangorn over the years, essentially forcing a mating on him. He wanted the children of a fae woman and a dragon shifter. Eilor felt that would allow him to harness the magic of the dragons. He obviously was a deeply suspicious man, because he hadn't even written down what it was he was seeking in the dragon magic.

Only that it was something he wanted, something he'd seen, and he felt he needed a child from the dragon shifter to access it.

The journals detailed numbers of women who were impregnated by Fangorn. Without fail, the women and babies died. Until Lionel. This particular son of Fangorn had lived. When Eilor told Lionel the truth about himself and Fangorn, Lionel found a way to escape. He'd run from the Dragon Realm, and Eilor hadn't been able to locate him for hundreds of years.

When Eilor received word that Lionel had finally been located, he was living in the Human Realm, and he'd married a human woman. At that time the woman, named Maria, was pregnant. Eilor had trapped the couple and brought them to the Dragon Realm. There, he'd separated them, and Maria had given birth to twins. To me, and to my brother, Aodan. After the birth, Lionel had been killed, or died—the journals weren't clear. Well, it was clear that Lionel no longer lived. Eilor hadn't gone into detail about how his death occurred. Maria—my mother—and Aodan disappeared. Eilor didn't know what happened, or he hadn't cared to note it.

At that point, he wasn't interested in a human woman who was already dying. The Fae Realm, in general, wasn't kind to humans. Nor was he interested in a boy. He wanted me, the girl.

Because he felt it would be a good thing to have Fangorn and I attempt to reproduce. The mere thought made me physically ill. I thought about the shifter I'd met a few times while Eilor was still in the castle. Eilor had always taken me to the cavern via portal, and he never portaled from the same place. Until recently, I'd had no idea where the cavern was, or how to get to it.

But while cleaning Eilor's former rooms, I'd found the entrance to the stairway that led to the dragon cavern. Of course, it was close to his rooms. It was a hidden door within the corridor that led to his rooms. It had a spell on it, and I'd found it by accident, as I'd found the journals. I'd spent my time so far just talking with Fangorn, getting to know him without the barrier of Eilor in the way. While I had no idea what he'd planned for Fangorn and me while he was alive, I'd always known it was something that wouldn't be for the benefit of anyone other than Eilor. So taking my time with Fangorn had been nice.

But today was the day I'd decided that I would go down, and see Fangorn again with an agenda. This time we were going to talk about my father. I'd left off pressing him on the issue. The one time I'd mentioned him, Fangorn's eyes had gone green, and he'd stopped talking for a while. So I'd not pressed him.

Today, however, it was going to happen. My grandfather. He knew I knew the truth. About who I was, where I'd come from, and what Eilor had planned for me. And the truth was horrible. It made me almost cry to think of it. I needed to change that narrative, and make what I knew something more than the horrors that Eilor had inflicted on my dragon family.

I wondered if Fangorn knew I was on a mission of sorts today. Somehow—I didn't know how—after I'd read the journals, he'd told me to come and find him. I'd heard his voice, in my head.

And then I'd found the entrance.

I thought it over. Taranath felt that there was a lot of wild magic in this Realm. The magic that was somehow connected to the land, to the dragons. That was the reason Eilor spent a lot of time studying it, trying to understand it so that he could harness it. His journals didn't indicate that he'd been successful. I thought Taranath was probably right. But I would find out more today; once I went to see Fangorn.

What did one wear to meet your grandfather, who was also a dragon, when you felt like you were going to pick a fight? The previous mention of my father had made him upset, or at least what I felt was him showing me that he was upset.

Before Drake and I had come here from the Fae Realm, Iris had given me a lot of clothing. I'd been wearing it more often than not, except when I was cleaning. Iris told me privately that dressing like I was somebody would help overcome my past in the Dragon Court. I'd been skeptical, but she'd been right. I noted that people who had known me for years treated me with greater courtesy and respect when I wore the clothing made for the Goblin Queen. Not that they knew that. All they knew was my clothing was exquisite, and well-made.

If it were good enough for the shifting sands of the Dragon Court, it would be good enough for my grandfather. Things had been tense between us since I'd brought Drake to see him. But I felt I had to. I had a responsibility to Drake, and why he was here, just as much as I assigned responsibility to myself for the safety of Fangorn and the other dragons. Even though Fangorn and I were not on solid footing, our relationship, while important, wasn't the only important thing. I hoped he could see that.

I put on a dress in dark purple that I felt made me look like the woman I aspired to be and tidied my hair. Jharak had mentioned, when I was still at the Fae Castle, that dragons loved formality. I'd always been so concerned with other things; not today. It couldn't hurt. It might make things a little easier. Finally, I could fiddle with my appearance no more, and I headed for the entrance down to the cavern.

The door slid open easily, cleverly concealed within what appeared to be a stone wall. I allowed it to shut behind me, and then took up the torch that was on the wall at the top of the long stairway. I'd asked Fangorn about being able to portal to him, as the stairway was a long one, but he wasn't sure how Eilor had managed it.

I hurried down, eager and nervous to talk to Fangorn. As I reached the bottom, I could see the torches in the cavern itself begin to light. They always did that once I was at the bottom.

"Grandfather?" I called.

A shuffling, and then a bright blue dragon lumbered forward from the back of the cell where Fangorn lived. In a cage. Like his brethren around him.

Wonderful. He was far less tactful in dragon form and far more straightforward. Perhaps I should wait—

"Daughter, I have felt your worry from the moment you opened the door above. What troubles you?"

Even though I wasn't his daughter, he told me it was dragon custom to call all your descendants 'son' or 'daughter.' As he'd lost all of his children in the dragon wars, he didn't stint with me in regards to traditions in the family department. I liked it.

"I want to talk to you about my parents, but I am nervous because you didn't seem interested in speaking about it the last time I asked you about them," I said, trying not to rush the words out. I found it much harder to sugar coat things with Fangorn when he was a dragon. "I also have some other news, but it can wait." I didn't want to tell him about Eilor just yet. That would derail any other conversation. He didn't speak right away. Then he let out a deep sigh, and I could see—and feel!—so much sorrow in that simple sound.

"Of course you want to know about them. I am sorry that I was not more welcoming, daughter. It's still difficult to talk of Lionel, even after—" he stopped. "You would imagine that after so much loss, after all the children I watched and felt grow, and then lost, that I would be able to speak of Lionel. But I find it a challenge." Another heavy sigh. "However, my feelings on the matter do not preclude your right to know. What do you wish to ask?"

That was far easier than I'd been expecting. "Well, what was he like? My father?"

I caught a bright green flash from Fangorn's eyes, and then they slanted in amusement. His eyes were green in both his fae and dragon forms, but they were like beacons when he was a dragon, especially when he was feeling a strong emotion, as he was now. I felt it radiating off him like rays from the sun.

"He was strong and very brave. Like me, he was not overly talkative, and once he learned that we were related, he and I were able to communicate. When Eilor told him the truth, I reached out to him with my thoughts, and he responded instantly. Even though I only saw him once more, we spoke all the time."

"Did you talk with him when Eilor brought him and my mother back?"

Fangorn's blue head nodded even before I'd finished my question. "Yes. I've known about you since before you were born. But Eilor threatened not only me, but you, and all the rest of our family," he let his head move to the left and the right to indicate the other ten sleeping dragons, "If I told you. I love you, daughter, as one last remaining members of my family. I could not, however, put them at risk."

"I understand. I wouldn't have wanted you to," I said. I meant it.

"Lionel told me about his life in the Human Realm. He was there for a long time, at least in human years. Several hundred years, if I am remembering correctly. He knew of all of his lost siblings, and he was careful never to mate and have children with any of the human women he kept company with. Until he met your mother. She was different, he said. He allowed me to see their meeting, and how their courtship progressed."

"You can do that?" I interrupted. I wasn't sure I wanted him to see inside my thoughts. There were too many that were jumbled and unsteady. This castle, my heritage, Drake—my mind slammed that thought away.

"I can if the other party chooses to allow me."

I couldn't deny how relieved that made me feel. "I'm sorry to interrupt. Please go on," I said.

His eyes crinkled at the corners, and I had the impression that he knew exactly what—or who—I was thinking about. He often did.

"Your father decided that he'd hidden long enough to be safe and to take the chance. He let himself fall in love and then told Maria the truth. Somehow, I am not sure how, she believed him, and they decided to start a family. You were very much wanted, daughter."

Hearing that brought tears to my eyes. I'd felt unwanted most of my life. To hear that my parents planned for me, wanted me—"What about Aodan? Can you feel him?"

Fangorn shook his head. "When your mother disappeared with him, I was no longer able to feel him. Eilor told me that he'd killed them, but I knew him well enough by then. She escaped somehow. I don't know how, but she managed it. I felt it when Lionel died." He looked away.

I didn't speak. I could see that my father's death still haunted him.

"To know that my son—the first son I'd had in hundreds of years, the son who almost got away, had died at the hands of the man who created nearly all of my misery—I very nearly broke the bars that day."

"What? I thought you couldn't break free!"

"I can't. That day was the closest I've ever come. To this day, I don't know why. But I nearly managed it that day. I couldn't, and my son died."

"I don't think you could have saved him. I've read the journals. Once he brought them here, my parents were not going to be able to live. If the baby—he didn't know there were twins when he brought them over—lived, my parents weren't important any longer. Plus," I added, thinking out loud, "Eilor wouldn't have wanted to deal with parents who might object to his awful plans."

Silence followed my words.

Then, "You are probably right. But to lose yet another child, when he'd grown and was an adult, and not be able to help him—my despair lasted until Eilor began to bring you to me. Only then did I realize that I had a chance to try and alter the course of the plans Eilor made. Thankfully, his daughter and the spawn of the Fae King set a different path in motion."

"I don't think Jharak claims Cian. Not as we knew him," I said before I could help it.

Fangorn was not an admirer of Jharak. He might be the only being I knew who didn't think the Fae King was marvelous.

"You cannot change who your family is. I am here because of who my family was. You are here for the same reasons. He may deny it all he wishes, that was still his son."

Fangorn lazily waved a claw at me as he continued. "I know we differ in our thoughts on the Fae King. I have no objection with that."

Then I remembered. "I also wanted to tell you that Eilor is dead."

"He is?" Fangorn sat up, and he began to shimmer in front of me. That meant that he was on the verge of shifting. For him to lose control like that meant that his emotions were very close to the surface, and very strong.

"That is where Drake just went. He got a message from Jharak that he'd found Eilor's body, and—"

"Where is the ring?" Fangorn demanded.

"I don't know. Drake hasn't returned yet. The dragon ring that Eilor wore?" I asked, seeing the ring in my mind's eye. "What's special about the ring?"

"It was crafted after the war. I helped to create it, so that the new Dragon King, and all that followed, would be part of the physical connection to this Realm. It was always so with the dragons. While I am not fond of the fae, I didn't want to see my land disappear entirely. I wanted to see the ties last. So I helped to craft a ring that would give a connection to the Realm itself to whichever Dragon King wore it."

I shrugged. "I don't know about the ring, but I'll ask Drake when he returns. What would you like me to tell him about it?"

"Bring the ring to me. I'll see if it is the actual ring or a false one. If it is indeed the king's ring, I will know that Eilor is dead. He would never let that ring away from him." Fangorn didn't hesitate.

"I will. Can I ask you for a favor, Grandfather?" Drake would be away for a while. I wanted something different right now. Just to forget, for a moment, that my entire world was in complete disarray.

"Of course."

"Could we speak of my father some more? I give you my word that I will speak to Drake when he returns, and I will bring the ring to you, but I would much rather talk of my father now if you don't mind," I said, hoping that I hadn't offended him.

He looked at me for what felt like a long moment, and then gave me his dragon approximation of a smile. "Of course, Aine. It is only natural that you wish to know of him."

With those words, he lay back down, curling into a comfortable sort of ball, a dragon ball, I thought, stifling the urge to laugh.

"Come and sit with me, and let's talk about family."

That was one thing I enjoyed about Fangorn in dragon form. He didn't dance around with his words. He'd told me that dragons were very direct, for the most part. That while they were wily, they didn't mince words or engage in small social talk.

Fangorn let his tail drift between the bars. I sat and leaned against the bars, and his tail came round to rest at my feet.

"Let me tell you of when I first became aware of him. I was aware of him long before he knew of me," Fangorn said, warmth in his voice.

The rumble of his words washed over me like a hot bath after a long day.

This was what it meant to have a family. I would protect Fangorn and the other dragons with my life. No one would take this family from me.

5

DRAKE

*H*e returned to his rooms, stretching as he did so. His manservant, Trevan, hurried in. "My lord, you're out and about late. May I get you anything? I was not sure where you were."

Drake heard the reproof in the man's tone. He debated as to whether or not this was appropriate, and then remembered the goblin woman who'd been the head of his staff. She had no problems treating him as an errant child.

"Trevan, I am sorry. The Fae King called for my assistance, and I needed to leave quickly. In the future, I will alert you if I need to leave suddenly."

"I mean no disrespect, My lord, but the Dragon Realm is not kind to...to those not from here."

"I am aware of that more each day," Drake said

dryly. "Accept my apologies for the unnecessary worry, and know that I shall not do it again."

Trevan nodded and began to help Drake remove his armor. Once he was in his night clothes once more, Trevan bowed and left the room. Which left Drake alone with his thoughts. He went and sat in one of the comfortable chairs in front of the fire, and pulled the ring from his pocket. He hadn't let Trevan see the ring. He didn't want to deal with any fallout of it showing up before the coronation. He'd need to get Taranath on this—

Blast. He'd promised to call Taranath. He went and found his mirror, and spoke, calling the mage. He sat down once more, idly going through some parchment he'd been working on earlier.

Taranath was at his door moments later, suggesting that the man had been waiting.

"I am glad to see you safely returned, My lord."

"Yes, that seems to be the sentiment. In addition to it's not safe for those not born here," Drake said, remembering Trevan's words.

"That's a fairly accurate statement, from what I can tell," Taranath said. "I also think that once you are crowned, and if the Realm accepts it—"

Drake held up a hand. "What do you mean, if the Realm accepts it?" Brennan said something similar when they were out collecting Eilor's mangy bones.

"This Realm, until Eilor, has always been ruled by dragons. Dragons are different than any other creature within the Realms. So is the Dragon Realm. It has, as one of its unique features, a connection to its ruler. This seems to be true for both dragon and fae. I have found texts that suggest in spite of line of succession, if the Realm didn't agree, the chosen dragon would not rule for long."

"Did these texts give any idea of how the Realm let everyone know?" Just what he needed. An opinionated Realm. As if there weren't enough challenges.

Taranath shook his head.

Drake threw up his hands. "Well, of course not! One more thing that falls under 'we'll need to wait and see what happens when we try to crown you, Drake! Oh, we're not worried! You can handle it!'"

"My lord," Taranath began.

"No, not to worry. All will be well. In the meantime, while we're waiting to see if the Realm or some nasty thing leftover from Eilor tries to maim or kill me, you need to have a look at this. I wouldn't touch it barehanded, however. It shocked my father."

He held out the ring, and Taranath took it, laying it in the long sleeve of the robes he wore. "What is it?"

"It's the ring of the Dragon King," Drake said with a sheepish grin, ashamed now of his outburst. It wasn't often his temper got the better of him. In spite of his reputation. "I am sorry for yelling," he started.

"No, My lord. No apology is necessary. This is a stressful time." Taranath smiled.

Drake wished again that he could keep Taranath. "See if any of that group of youngsters has any talent, and start sorting out who might be a good, trustworthy candidate for Court Mage. I'll need to let you go eventually, and I need a mage I can trust who also understands this Realm. No one with a secret yearning for the old king, either!"

"I think we are safe on that score, My lord. All those who even seemed sympathetic to Eilor have been sent home on regional missions," Taranath replied.

"What is a regional mission?" Drake asked, intrigued in something other than his own troubles.

"It's a go home and stay out of the Court assignment," Taranath grinned. "Not called that, of course, and touted as a grave responsibility. But I don't need questionable loyalties at this point. Nothing to worry over, My lord. I will have a good candidate for you before I leave. If I may, I'll leave you now."

Drake rubbed his eyes with his thumb and forefinger, hoping he wouldn't get another headache. "Yes, of course. Come and let me know the moment you find anything, anything at all."

Taranath nodded and quietly left. The click of the door latch was the only sign of his leaving.

The way Taranath moved suggested he'd been trained in more than just magic. But he was completely trustworthy, and whatever had given him the stealth and grace that he had, Drake was grateful for it.

His mind still whirred, although his eyelids were heavy. He thought over the planning going on right now for the coronation. He hadn't been lying when he told his father and Brennan that he had no idea how Eilor hadn't starved. Outside of the usual tyrant's behavior of high taxes, and feeding and adorning himself and family however they wished, Eilor showed no signs of ever considering that his people would suffer.

Drake liked to think that it was his capable, warrior self who would lead the charge and restore the Realm. He feared it would be the organizational, get-things-done attitude that would be the reason the Realm moved into a better place; that moved the Realm away from the sickness Eilor inflicted upon it for so long. Even more outrageous, he found that he didn't mind being the person who got things moving as they needed to be.

Which brought him back round to where he'd been before Jharak called. The planning of the coronation. It was a coronation, not the coming of some mystical being. But given the intensity of the headache he was getting from all the planning, or more importantly, the planners, it may well be.

He wondered again, for the umpteenth time, why he'd agreed to do this.

Because he couldn't tell his father no. That was it, put simply. He couldn't tell Jharak no.

Although in fairness, he didn't know many who could. Even Iris, Brennan's human-born queen, who hadn't grown up with the man, wasn't immune to Jharak's charm.

It was no surprise that Jharak's son wouldn't have the ability to say no, either.

After all the dead had been taken care of due to Cian's attempts to kill his entire family, Jharak had moved immediately to the management of the mess that was left behind by all the troublesome denizens who had supposedly been running the Dragon Realm.

Jharak's solution? To have Drake assume the throne of the Dragon Realm. To have Drake be a king. He'd never wanted a crown, a throne, a lifetime of responsibility for so many.

But because he couldn't say no, here he was. And fool that he was, he thought this would be easy. After all, working together with Brennan, they'd been able to sort out all the problems of the Goblin Realm for the past six hundred years, give or take a decade. How bad could the Dragon Realm be?

Drake leaned forward, rubbing his forehead with his fingers. He'd had to ask the question, hadn't he? Now the question was, *How much worse could it get?*

When he and Aine had come here, after the fight in the Fae Castle he'd been under duress. Extreme duress. He'd been sure that after a month, he'd tell Brennan and his father, thanks for the chance, but this wasn't going to happen. That he, Drake, wasn't fit to be a king, and couldn't manage it, nor did he want to rule a realm.

But then Aine had found Eilor's journals. He shuddered at the thought of what they'd learned from the journals. Most of all, after he got past his anger, Drake felt sorry for Aine. In spite of the odd way he felt after being around her for any length of time, he couldn't ignore her suffering. She deserved better. The entire Realm did.

Not that he'd tell her.

She'd do her best to skewer him.

Aine had been convinced that Eilor wasn't dead. Drake, along with his father, and Brennan, wasn't as sure. Until tonight, anyway. Now he knew Eilor was dead. Why didn't he feel any sense of relief?

Before tonight, he agreed with Aine that the man must have skipped out of the Realm; done a runner after the death of his daughter and his pet killer, Cian. But Drake hoped that Eilor had died while trying to get away and failing. The vision of that monster dying in reach of something he wanted felt extremely satisfying.

It would have been more satisfying to run a blade through Eilor in a public square, but Drake wasn't picky. Dead was dead. Dead was gone.

A provably dead Eilor would make his life a lot easier. He hoped that Jharak would make the announcement soon. As it was, the specter of Eilor hung over the castle, in spite of the efforts of himself, Aine, and Taranath to clean things out, make the Dragon Castle, and the Dragon Realm better.

Taranath had arrived first, the day after the deaths of Cian and Ailla.The mage had promptly announced that the old king was gone and that the Fae King's Regent, Drake, would be arriving shortly. There was a delay because Drake had to be talked—pushed, was more like it—into it.

What decided him that he would stay, and what he would admit to no one else, even then, before he knew of the journals, was Aine. She'd risked a great deal to help Brennan when Cian kidnapped him, and she was fervently committed to helping the dragons trapped within the Dragon Realm. While she hadn't known how to get to them at that time, she'd been sure she would figure it out. And she had. Ever since she'd found the door to the dragons' cavern, she'd been visiting Fangorn regularly.

Until she'd shown him Eilor's journals, Drake hadn't believed the dragons were trapped. They were contained, as they'd been after the great wars over a thousand years before. Wars that had been started by the dragons, and their quest for power.

There were only eleven dragons left. Of that eleven, ten were asleep. They'd been asleep so long; it wasn't a sure thing they could ever be woken. Drake wasn't sure that waking them up would be a good idea.

Jharak had shared with him and Aine that the dragons who remained were the more reasonable, less war-like of their race, but that wasn't saying a great deal. Not when it came to dragons. They were ferocious even when calm.

But Drake had seen Aine after she found Eilor's journals. He could see how devastated she was. He realized then that while the dragons needed to be contained, they were, in fact, trapped. Fangorn most of all had been made to suffer in ways that weren't appropriate, even if his kind needed to feel the consequences of starting a war.

And seeing how Aine reacted was what did it for Drake in regards to making his decision. Aine, who'd grown up in a truly loveless, tortuous world with only

Eilor as anything resembling a parent cried when she read the journals. Her tears weren't only for herself. The journals hurt her to read, she'd told him. But they didn't break her. Aine was just as determined to carry out her goals.

Drake had decided that if she could take the blows that such knowledge afforded, that in spite of Eilor, it was worth it to try and salvage this Realm. Because Aine had been at the center of being raised by a madman. And she was still focused, honest, and honorable.

There had to be hope for the rest of the Realm, too. It made Drake feel that what this Realm needed was a chance, a fair shot at being what it could.

So he'd told Jharak that he would accept the throne. The planning had begun in earnest. Which brought him here, three days away from his coronation. With only the slight diversion of a dead king and a possible killer ring to divert him from the madness. Oh, and a potentially persnickety Realm.

Nothing at all to worry about.

He thought about Aine and the dragons some more. It was nice to focus on someone else's problems for a bit.

When Aine had finally found the entrance to the cavern with the dragons' cages, he'd been excited that she was taking him to see them. But seeing them was different than imagining them. Up close, even asleep, they radiated power.

Fangorn, the dragon fae shifter, scared Drake in a way he'd never been scared before. The weight of the shifter's gaze, the intensity that showed in even the smallest of actions—he was glad there were only eleven left. What must it have been like, facing an entire Realm full of dragons? He didn't even want to think about it.

Back to the coronation. The problems of the—soon to be his—Realm weren't going anywhere. They would still be present and demanding attention three days from now. All Drake had to do was get through the next two days, and then his father would take over for a bit. All he needed to do was go where told. There would be a fairly large celebration. Once that concluded, he could get back to work.

Work that included finding out what else Eilor had been up to and who his conspirators were that might be left within the Realm. There had to be some. Taranath had shown that with the arrangements he'd made for those suspected of harboring sympathy for Eilor.

Which brought him back to his original worry. There was far too much fuss going on here. That was even given the fact that his mother, normally the head of any fussing, wasn't part of this at all. He hoped he hadn't dug his own grave by insisting she show up and put a good face on things.

The thought that she was still sulking over someone who had tried to end all of them made him angry as he felt when he considered Eilor and what he knew of the man. Cian had been no better.

The man Cian was nothing like the son she'd remembered. Cian had planned to kill even her, his mother. Drake felt no guilt that he'd been part of the death of Cian. But Nerida didn't see it that way. Drake found that he was both hurt and angry when he thought of her. He'd never disagreed with her in this manner before. He hoped some peace could be found because this felt wretched. But it would need to come from Nerida, and that day would be a long day coming from his mother.

Drake pushed the thought of Nerida aside. He couldn't worry about her now.

The door burst open. No knock, he noticed.

Aine rushed in with excitement on her face. Given that she was normally fairly calm, Drake set down the parchment he was trying to read.

"Come right in, Aine."

6

DRAKE

*A*ine threw herself into the chair across from him, ignoring his sarcasm. "I'm glad you're back. I have been down talking with Fangorn."

Drake restrained himself from rolling his eyes. Of course, she was talking with the dragon. She spent a lot of time there. From a selfish point of view, he wanted to point out that her desire to talk with Fangorn was taking away from the work she was supposed to be doing with Taranath to get this Realm up and running. But he didn't have the heart to scold her. Nor did he have the right, although he dearly wanted to.

Besides, if he let himself get angry with Aine, he would have to examine the idea that he was just mad because she wasn't doing what he wanted. That idea in and of itself was troubling, and he didn't want to think about it. It made him worry that he'd already morphed into a demanding and selfish ruler. So he let her do what she felt she needed, and accepted the time and help she was willing to give regarding the Dragon Realm.

"What did he have to say?"

"I told him of your leaving. He doesn't think Eilor is dead."

That made Drake sit up. "There is no need to tell the dragon everything that goes on," he said stiffly. Her words brought back Jharak's concerns. How could he be sure she was on his side of things?

Regarding Eilor, he'd seen the body. Did Fangorn still have contact with Eilor? Was there some plot in the works that he was deciding to confess? His mind raced with the possibilities.

"He says that he has been focused on Eilor for so long that he can sense him. He says that it's still there —the sense of Eilor, I mean. But…" She frowned.

"What?"

"He says that Eilor is not in this Realm."

Now Drake did roll his eyes. "Well, of course not. Why would he be? I don't know for sure where those who die go, but they don't stay here."

"Cian hid in this Realm for hundreds of years." Aine shot back, one of her eyebrows arching.

Drake opened his mouth, then closed it. Then he

sighed. "You have a point. Hiding in plain sight is often a good tactic. Particularly when people don't expect it. But I have one reason why that won't work."

Her eyes narrowed. "Why?"

"I saw the body. And we have the Dragon King's ring."

Her eyes narrowed. "We haven't found Niles."

Niles. Another thing to worry about. Niles, according to Aine, and some of the staff that was beginning to open up to him was the closest thing Eilor had to a second in command. He'd disappeared by the time Taranath had gotten to the castle. But he was not gone, as Drake had cause to know. He just wasn't anywhere that Drake could get to him, and cut his heart out.

As Taranath had arrived only one day after the death of Cian and Ailla, Niles being able to escape was a testament for how quickly news could spread. It made Drake uneasy to think that someone from the Fae Castle might have been part of it.

But it was also the manner in which news spread. Fast, and when you didn't want it to. Servants talked all over the Realms.

"I think there's a larger number of people sympathetic to Eilor than just Niles," he began. He didn't want to think about the coronation, or anything else.

"I agree with you," Aine said.

Drake held up a hand. "To that end, based on my conversations, Taranath's work, and your snooping and years here, I've come up with two—no, three—lists." He stood, going over to the desk where he kept his private papers and pulled the piece of parchment he'd been working on earlier in the evening from the pile and offered it to her.

"What are they?" Aine asked, taking the parchment without looking at it immediately.

"They are my lists of one, who I can trust. Two, who I don't believe I can trust. And three, those whom I am unsure of. You'll notice," his mouth twisted in annoyance, "that the first list is abysmally short, and the third very long."

She looked at the parchment then. Drake could see her reading it, her eyes stopping now and then at one name or another. Then her eyes met his, and she smiled.

"At least there are people on the first list."

"Well, of course. I brought some of them with me. Never mind that—tell me what you think?"

He waited to see what she would say. She often brought him the news he wouldn't have discovered any other way. It wasn't often the best of news, but he appreciated that she was such a good source of information.

7

DRAKE

*D*rake found that he relied more on Aine than he'd ever thought he would. He was very grateful now she'd wanted to come back, even if she did have her own very prominent agenda. He hadn't known initially how helpful she would be.

She knew the Dragon Realm. She knew the people. Because she'd been someone who wasn't completely accepted within the court structure but had been raised there, she saw a lot. Probably more than the courtiers in this Realm realized.

Drake had seen the way the courtiers reacted to her. It was Aine said—with fear, some with varying degrees of loathing. She was too much connected to Eilor and the things he was doing that no one really knew about. Well, they all knew he was doing something, and it had to do with the dragons, but that was all people knew. They speculated wildly. He'd heard some pretty incredible things. Aine was given a great deal more skill and power than she had.

He looked at her again. Or were the rumors true? Had she merely kept some of her skills from him? From Jharak? Was she withholding? He would say no, but he couldn't be sure.

Nevertheless, he'd put her name on his list of people he could trust. No sense in making a fight where it wasn't necessary. Drake always loved a fight, but he seemed to have so many at the moment, he found he didn't want to start anymore.

She read through each list carefully and then looked up at him. "This is a good start. We can go through this later when you have more time. Right now," She smiled, "Your Majesty, you need to get ready for your guests." She held out the lists to him

Drake took them and leaned back in his chair, groaning. They were back to the coronation. His father, Brennan, and Iris, and a host from the Fae Realm were due to descend shortly. All witnesses who were being brought here so that Jharak could be seen to crown him, and then throw a big party. So that everything looked fine.

Jharak felt, and Drake agreed, that if there were people with different ideas, they'd come forward at that point. He didn't get the impression that many would be sad to see Eilor displaced. He hoped that he was correct in that assumption. There were so many unknowns that faced you when you were the leader.

Something he'd not fully appreciated even as Brennan's right-hand man all those years.

Just in case Drake was overly optimistic, Taranath had assigned all of the remaining mages to help guard the Dragon Castle while the festivities were at hand. Everyone was on alert. Well, everyone close to him.

The people of the castle and most of the courtiers seemed happier, though. Which reminded him —"What is the mood about the place?"

She shrugged. "The same. Lots of chatter over clothing, and the cooks are going spare at the thought of the Fae King under their roof. I wouldn't go to the kitchens for the next few days," Aine finished with a grin.

"Noted. Have you seen any signs of a plot?"

She barked a short, derisive laugh. "Do you mean have I seen anyone huddling in corners, or waving a stone or some other magical aid in your direction while muttering under their breath? Be reasonable, Drake. The people we need to worry about are far more subtle than that!"

"Allow me a little latitude here, please. I've never had to plan a coronation, or run a kingdom, or throw a damnable party before!" Drake stood, knocking papers off his desk. He knew this would make his life more difficult when he came back to it, but at the moment, he didn't care.

"I'm not a mage! There's no waving of my hand to make all these things happen! And everyone! EVERYONE! Comes to me, sure that their problem is one that only I can solve. I can, but so could others. No one goes to them. They're all right here, knocking on my door! At all hours!" Drake gestured at the door to his chambers. "I get no peace! No rest! No time to do anything! Not even here, when I am available all during the day in my study!"

He stepped away from out from around his desk, not wanting to make even more work for himself later. "I've got to solve the mystery of what is going on with the king's ring, plan this thing my father insists on, and *then* hope his cronies don't try and up and kill all my family in addition to killing me. My family, by the way, who believes that I am my normal, paranoid, overly cynical self." He threw up his hands.

"Then there's the little issue of a herd of dragons camped out in the cellar! What do I do with them, hey? I don't know! You want...I don't even know what you and Fangorn want, although as much time as you spend together, I would think that not only have you had the chance to figure that out, but that you might be good enough to tell me!"

He looked back at his lists in her hands, his frustration making him nearly grind his teeth. What was he going to do with these people? He itched to grab it from her and toss it onto the desk. Staring at the lists wouldn't answer his questions, or solve anything. The rising anger and frustration he'd felt speaking with Taranath reared its head once more, and he found it difficult to keep it at bay.

Over the last month, he'd felt better about his place within the Realm. But the more he learned, the more people opened up and spoke with him, the more he realized he was going to need help. The very reason that he was here was that Jharak needed help. But how could he know who to trust? How was he to know who he could entrust with his concerns and his fears and... And his Realm?

That was a staggering thought. His Realm. He never considered himself as having a Realm that was his and within three short days, he would. People were already starting to call him *Your Majesty.* He kept looking around, expecting to see his father or Brennan. At least he'd managed to curb that impulse in the last week or so. Which was a good thing, as it was starting to get a little embarrassing? Even worse, he hadn't noticed he was doing it until Aine pointed it out.

And somehow, without even trying, he'd come back to Aine again. He wasn't sure she was a problem, but she kept looming as one. She would be ideal to trust, but Drake knew that the concerns of the Realm were not her primary focus. Not only that, he wondered why she'd seen him looking for what he considered the real kings when no one else had noticed. He wasn't sure what he thought of her watching him. Why was she doing it?

As though she could read his thoughts, she looked up from the lists she was cafefully studying. "Did you say something?"

He stifled a sigh. He could tell she'd been giving him time to gather himself together, so that he was no longer ranting like an angry child. "No. Well, I don't know. I might have begun talking to myself. I was thinking. But pay me no mind. It's just the muttering of a man going mad."

Aine rolled her eyes. "And here I thought your family were the ones given to greater fits of drama. It seems you are too, My lord."

"You do know I'm about to be the king?" Drake asked, wincing internally at how much he sounded like his brother, Brennan. Formal, and stuffy. Was this what being a king did to one?

Aine laughed outright and then gave him that small smile that he thought of as particularly hers and sat down in a chair across from him again. Drake took a deep breath and hoped for calm and rational thought. Her smile warmed him from within. He couldn't think about such things right now.

"All right," he said, "Let's focus on one thing at a time. Back to Eilor, and his body. How does Fangorn suggest we know for sure? Since my seeing it with my own eyes is not proof enough." Drake resisted the urge to roll his eyes.

"In speaking with Fangorn, he asked a very good question that's also part of why he doesn't believe Eilor is dead. And it's one that I have not seen the answer to."

"And?" He asked.

"Why is it that Jharak and Brennan believe the body you saw was truly Eilor?"

"Other than seeing the body, he was wearing the dragon ring. Did you ever see him without it?" Drake waited for her response, and Aine shook her head. "I thought so. Additionally, Jharak wants to put a new king in place, and that story works with his narrative." Drake ground out.

Aine laughed again. "It's good to see that you still have the capacity to joke," she said. "Where is the ring, and where is Eilor's body?"

"Well, we haven't shared this as of yet, but we found him on the border of three Realms, and he appeared to be the victim of multiple stab wounds, " Drake said.

Aine nodded her head. "He mentioned the ring. That's a good sign for Eilor's being dead. Fangorn also shared with me today that the cages are connected somehow to the King of the Dragon Realm. That neither he, nor I, nor anyone else can open the cages. If the King who sets the lock is still alive, based on what Eilor told Fangorn over the years," she said. "The cages don't budge. They remain locked."

Drake held up a hand. "Wait a minute," he said, trying to process everything that she just told him. "You're telling me that the cages down in that cavern were locked however long ago by Eilor? Am I hearing this correctly?" She nodded and opened her mouth. He held up his hand a little higher, "Wait. Let me finish. I'm just a single-minded warrior, and don't think in the many layers like you dragons."

She sat back in her chair and crossed her arms, one brow raised, and waiting.

"And since Eilor set the cages to be locked, he is the only one that can unlock them? Is that what you are telling me? In addition to the idea that Fangorn says he can still sense Eilor?"

Aine nodded, and said, "Yes. Fangorn says that while Eilor is still the king, there is no way to open those cages."

Drake frowned. "So to Fangorn, there is no doubt that Eilor lives still?"

Aine nodded yes again.

Why had he thought that dealing with Aine's dragon concerns would be easier? He leaned back in his chair, lacing his hands behind his neck. He went over Brennan's words about the ring, and why it hadn't shocked Drake when it had shocked Jharak. "Could it be a matter that there is no Dragon King at the moment? The old King is dead, but there is no new King? That only the Dragon King can undo the locks?"

At this, Aine looked unsure. "I asked something like that. Fangorn himself is not sure, either. All he knows is what Eilor told him."

Drake held up both hands. "Wait just a moment! He's basing this off of what Eilor told him? We already know that Eilor would lie about the sky being blue. Why does Fangorn think that Eilor was telling the truth? This one moment in time?"

For a moment, Drake thought that she was going to argue with him further. But instead, he could tell she was thinking about his words.

"It's a good question," she said. "I don't know. And in all honesty, Drake, Fangorn doesn't know either. While we have the journals—"

"You've taken them down to show Fangorn?" Drake jumped on that one immediately.

The journals were another source of constant argument. Mostly, because while Drake regarded them as proof of living horror, and he felt, even while he wanted to protect Aine's privacy, he wanted to share them with Taranath. At least the mage could be helpful.

But Aine resisted. She didn't want them close to her, so she'd given them to Drake for safe keeping. But she also refused to let him share them. He respected her wishes, but at the same time...Drake sighed. The damn journals. At least she'd not been rifling in his room, toting the journals back and forth to Fangorn.

When cleaning out Eilor's rooms, Aine found three leather-bound journals that detailed all that Eilor had been doing to make his very own army made up of fae dragon shifters. Aine was a result of that.

The journals laid it all out in stark horror.

Since she'd discovered them, Aine's focus had shifted. She still helped him, but she was very intent on helping the dragons. Her family, he thought.

Which was understandable, but her occasional lack of availability made it clear to Drake how much he counted on her. He couldn't decide if her secrecy or his own dependence on her annoyed him more.

Aine smiled, faintly. "Why would I need to? He was there for the things that happened. Most of them happened to or because of him. He understands my concerns."

"But you'll talk about them with Fangorn?" He knew he sounded petty. He couldn't help it.

Aine seemed to be struggling with some inner emotion. Finally, her expression smoothed out and she said, "Fangorn is my grandfather, Drake. Fangorn has been the focus of Eilor's horrific actions for thousands of years. He's lost many children, many women that he cared for. I'm all that he has left. And..." She looked down at her hands.

Instinctively, Drake knew he needed to keep his mouth shut. It was rare to see Aine discomfited like this. So he kept his mouth shut and waited.

Still looking at her hands, Aine continued, "I'm ashamed. I'm ashamed of how I came to be. You don't understand; you can't! When I read those journals, I can see, I can feel the way that Fangorn felt, the way those women felt, the loss of so many babies! I know fae aren't supposed to cry, and I have no idea about dragons, but I weep like Iris when I read those journals."

He knew that she didn't mean any insult when she compared herself to Iris. More she compared herself to Iris' human ability to cry at what seemed like at will. Even more so now that Iris was pregnant.

"I wish you told me this before, Aine. I wouldn't

badger you about it so much if I'd known I was causing actual distress," Drake said, feeling as low as he could get.

"Don't blame yourself, Drake. I have not been willing to share this much with anyone, but I can't keep it to myself any longer."

"You really believe you're something to be ashamed of?" He asked her, hating that she might feel this way.

Aine looked at him and shrugged her shoulders helplessly. "I don't know. *I don't know.* There is so much that I don't know. That Fangorn doesn't know. And while you have given these journals some mythical status, they are not. They are a log of all the things that Eilor did, a log of his victims, and of all the pain he caused. I can't bear to look at them, which is why I have given them to you for safe keeping."

"None of that is your fault, Aine. It might help if you allowed me, or my father to read the journals, to share the burden," Drake said. He didn't want her taking on any more guilt than she already felt. Not that he knew the level of guilt she might be feeling. He realized then that he was very interested to know what she felt. He found, in spite of all the things pressing on him that he wanted to continue this conversation.

The problem being, he didn't do feelings. He didn't do any of that sort of thing well. Hack at things with a sword, and he was the fae to get that done.

"How can it not be my fault? I'm what he was after. Even worse, I have a twin out there somewhere, and I don't know what happened to him."

Drake thought she was optimistic in thinking the boy was still alive. But he wouldn't tell her that. He also noted that she'd dodged answering his request to share them with Jharak. *Oh, well Father. I tried.* "Do you think your twin still alive? He was very young when he disappeared with your mother." He couldn't help asking.

Aine had shared that when Eilor had discovered that somehow, Maria and one of the babies had gotten away, he'd written how thankful he was that he had the girl because she was the more valuable of the twins. Drake wondered if that was part of her guilt as well.

"I don't know what to think. I've never had any sense of another person or any of those things that you hear about twins being able to share."

Twins were extremely rare in the Fae Realm. Drake could only think of two instances in his nearly seven hundred years where a fae woman gave birth to twins. Children were rare enough with fae women. Twins had almost a mythical status. He'd heard they could read each other's minds, but that might just be gossip because they were not something that occurred regularly.

He didn't want to talk about things like this that

there were no answers for. All it did was make him feel bad with no end in sight. And it took a toll on Aine. She hid it, but he could see it on her. She looked so sad; he wanted to...what was he thinking? Time to focus.

"So what does any of this have to do with Eilor being dead?" He decided that the best bet was to bring things back to the question at hand.

8

AINE

I stared at him, unable to believe the switch of the direction of the conversation. I finally decided to trust him, and he wanted to focus on Eilor? And the journals? And everything else outside of what I'd just shared with him?

What was it Iris had said the last time we'd spoken? "Men," and she'd rolled her eyes. That statement seemed to cover this situation as well.

I sighed. "Because if Eilor is not truly dead, then all of the things that he was attempting to do are still things that he's going to attempt to do. His goals are not going to change, Drake. Not after all this time." Was he really this simple? I'd always thought he was fairly intelligent, but sometimes, in conversations like this, I found that I wondered.

"In defense of my father and brother, and even my humble, less-learned self, the body we found was convincing. There were items that were identified as being Eilor's, and he had a bag of things that someone would take when they were fleeing. We also have the ring." Drake offered an explanation that I wasn't sure even he believed.

To my ears, it almost sounded as though Drake wasn't going to entertain questions about the matter. In spite of what I just told him. In spite of the fact he wasn't sure he agreed. I thought about how to say this in a way that would get through his thick skull.

"I understand that, but he didn't take his journals. He didn't even try to come back here and retrieve them. Those books represent a thousand years of work and planning on his part. And the magic that was used on the dragon cells would suggest that there are other theories that ought to be explored," I said.

Drake frowned, his lips pursing together hard. I'd learned, over the past two months that this meant he was thinking about what someone said to him, even though he didn't want to admit they might be right. He was very funny to watch at times. Very set in his ways, very much used seeing the world through the lenses of a warrior, things in black-and-white. Some of the biggest bursts of frustration that I saw from him or when things going on here in the Court had to be dealt with, and there was no clear-cut answer. Case in point with his outburst earlier.

People looked to him to provide a clear-cut answer. Even if he wasn't formally the king, he was the king in the ways that mattered. So it frustrated him when he couldn't give a solution, a clear-cut answer to a problem. Personally, I found it rather endearing. Drake exuded competence and that he was a capable and strong man. I thought it fitting that he was named Drake. That was another term for a dragon. No dragon is easily tamed, I thought. Especially the Dragon Realm.

"All right. So Fangorn does not believe that Eilor is dead. I can see why he'd think so. Where does he think he went then?"

It was nice to see the Drake had at least decided to humor me. I gave the question serious thought.

"While he can't be sure, and you're right, this is based on the idea that Eilor was telling the truth. So while he cannot be sure, he feels like if Eilor were truly dead, I should have been able to open the door to his cell."

The most extraordinary expression came over his face. It was amazement, then shock, and finally, anger. I sighed.

"I must stop here, and ask for clarification, Aine. Are you telling me that you tried to set Fangorn free?"

"Of course I did. If you were in a cage, I wouldn't just leave you there were it within my power to let you out."

Drake opened his mouth and then closed it. Got up, and looked out the window. I stayed silent.

He turned to face me. I'd rarely seen such a serious expression on his face. "You should have told me that you were going to try. That you had tried. That Fangorn asked you to free him."

"He didn't ask me. I offered!" I also didn't tell him the test was only the first time, and I'd tried several times since then.

"Oh, of course, he didn't ask you! No, he wouldn't. He would just put it out there, and let you come to the idea on your own. Aine! The dragons nearly destroyed all the Realms when they were free before!"

"He's not going to do anything! He's been in a cage, forced to breed and see his children and the women he cared for die for a thousand years! Wouldn't you want to be free?" I shouted. It was either shout or cry, and I wasn't going to cry in front of Drake. Not now.

"Of course I would. But I'm not from the race that nearly ended all the Realms. Fangorn is. That's something else entirely, outside of keeping someone locked up. Now, as for what it will take to open the cages," Drake tapped his fingers on his face. "It's not the worst idea ever," he said, leaning back in his chair again. I could see that he was thinking this over. "There is logic to it. It makes sense. But there is something more, and I'd like you to ask him about it."

"Okay," I said. "It's not going to be insulting, is it?" I was focusing on keeping my temper. It wouldn't help Fangorn or me if I lost it. The last time I had brought Drake down to the cavern, he'd irritated Fangorn to no end. And the irritation had been mutual. I didn't understand it. We were on the same side. But I didn't have time to worry about the egos of two men who thought highly of themselves. One man, and one dragon.

"No, I'm not trying to be insulting at all," he said, looking at me earnestly. "I am wondering if there needs to be a new king who countermands the orders of the old King. Someone who is taking the crown shortly," he finished with a grin.

I thought about it. It was not the worst idea ever, and it did have logic behind it. "So what you're saying is...?"

"That not only must the old king be gone, but there must be a new king on the throne." Drake finished for me, nodding. "So until both pieces of this are met, whatever is needed to counteract Eilor's spells won't come into place until after there's a new Dragon King. That not only does there need to be a crowned King, but he has to be accepted by the Realm and have the ring.."

"You know, Drake, sometimes you're more than just a warrior with the sword," I said, smiling. I stood up. "Will you talk to your father, and Brennan this? About whether there is any room for doubt in their beliefs? Will you explain to them what it is that Fangorn has expressed to me?"

"It would be better if you would allow Jharak or Brennan to come and speak with Fangorn themselves," he said, and I could see his displeasure.

Today was obviously the day to go over things already stated.

"He's not ready for visitors, nor am I." I glared at him. We had this conversation. More than once. I thought I'd been pretty clear on my intentions. The last time we spoke about it after Drake had been down with me to see Fangorn. Which was only three days ago. Yet he seemed to have completely forgotten our conversation.

"He's going to have to be ready at some point, Aine. He can't hide out down there forever. What happens when the cages do open? Then, not only will Fangorn be free, but the other ten dragons will be free as well."

I took two steps closer to the desk, leaning onto it so that I could make my point very clear. "We don't even know that those dragons will wake up, Drake!

Fangorn told me he hadn't seen them awake since many years ago, and that he can barely even feel them anymore."

"Part of being a king is anticipating all outcomes," he said coldly. He knew that irritated me. It did so now. Which irritated me further. I should be able to resist these petty behaviors. And the fact that Drake and I already had patterns as to how we argued.

"The dragons are not going to harm us again!" I said, leaning over the desk.

Drake may not have understood the art of diplomacy as well as other kings, but he understood the art of warfare. He knew what I was trying to do, and he stood up so that he now loomed over me. Rather than the other way around. Damn the man!

"You don't know that, Aine. You wish you hope it. But you don't know it. I've only been down to speak with Fangorn twice, and I can feel the sheer power coming off of the man! And he's *only* in his fae form, not even in his dragon form. What do you think he would be capable of as a dragon?"

"I think that Fangorn has seen enough of how things are, and how they could be, that he's not going to allow things to get to the point where they were!" I was thinking of when Fangorn and I had talked about his children.

Not just the children that Eilor had forced him to

breed. Fangorn had children that were full dragons, children that were alive before the great war of the dragons against the rest of the Realms.

We had spoken of them several more times, and each time he opened up a little more. At the time of the war, he had seventeen children, with three other female dragons. Apparently, dragons were not into mating with just one dragon and sticking together as a couple.

All the female dragons and all seventeen of his children had perished in the great war. He admitted, and I could hear what it took for him to make such an admission, that they had all been very much in favor of the war. And that had they lived; they would not have been able to live within the barriers of peace.

"How is it that you were allowed to live, what with all of your family being so in favor of the war?" I'd asked him.

"Because it was well known that I had opposed the war. My children and all of my mates shunned me. They felt I was a traitor to our race. But I watched the fae carefully. They were capable of adapting, and of change. We dragons are strong, and our magic is even more so. We do not change well. We do not manage adaptation well. We are a race that forces people and animals and things around us to adapt. We do not adapt. And I think that was our downfall."

The sadness in his words and the look on his face were with me as I stood here in this office with Drake.

"According to Fangorn, the dragons that were allowed to live were those among them who actively spoke against the war, who attempted to dissuade the rest of the dragons from beginning the conflict in the first place."

Drake laughed, and it wasn't a happy or nice laugh. "The least warlike among them? Do you hear yourself? Dragons by nature are warlike, and they are selfish, and they don't wish to share with others, and they are greedy. That's why so many of our kind died in the great war."

"Our kind? Drake, I am both fae and dragon! So, all kinds are my kind! And I have no family on the side of the fae, and one relative from my dragon side? That kind of argument won't work with me."

"It should work with you! You are accepted as fae —!"

I slammed my hand on the table. It was very satisfying, in spite of the sting on the palm of my hand. "No, I am not accepted in the world of the fae! I've been very clear about why I could not come back here and run the Dragon Realm on my own. People do not trust me. They don't know why, as Eilor never said anything one way or another about me other than I was his ward. What they do know there's something different about me, something not quite right. Don't tell me the fae accept me! I'm not accepted at all! Were you not here, I truly believe they would've cast me out."

Drake was taken aback by my vehemence. "You can't know that Aine," he began.

I leaned over with the emphasis of the point I was trying to make. "Oh yes, I can! You don't hear the whispers; you haven't grown up hearing the whispers as I have my entire life!"

Now Drake leaned forward on the desk, leaning down slightly so that he could glare at me eye to eye. "You think I don't know about questions and whispers? I am the human-born son of the Fae King! You are how old, Aine? You don't know a thing about whispers and pointing and people talking. Barely even waiting until you pass them." He stood up, looking into the distance.

Then he looked at me again. "What are you? Five and twenty? Perhaps thirty? I've been in the Fae Realm for six hundred and fifty years! I've had to hear, *he's only a human more* than you've woken in the morning! Don't tell me I don't know what it means to be pointed at and whispered at and referred to in the most common, hurtful terms possible!"

I could tell that I angered him at this point. He turned and went to stand at his window, a sure sign of that anger.

But I wasn't giving up on this. "At least people knew what you are! And now, regardless of what they say, you're fae, Drake. You may have begun life as a human, you may have lived here as a human for some time, but you are fae, nothing else. You're about to become the Dragon King! If people say anything at all anymore, they will whisper it, hoping not to be caught! People barely even cover their mouths or lower their voices as I pass by! They assume the worst about Eilor, and they assume that I'm part of whatever was that he was doing that was the absolute worst thing possible! Don't compare yourself to me! We are not the same."

Drake whirled around, and I could tell that he had truly lost his temper.

"Oh, so this is to be a 'whose life is worse' discussion? Are we going to compare notes and see who suffered more? Do you hear yourself, Aine?"

"I do hear myself!" I could feel my temper rising as well. I worked very hard to keep it to a low-key response to everything. It didn't happen this time. "While you may feel that other fae look down on you, and foolishly, some of them might, you are known. You are understood. I am not. Worse than that, I am something unknown, a part of something that Eilor was doing in secret. Which can only be bad." I took a breath, willing the damned tears to stay put and not spill down my cheeks.

Then I continued. It needed to be said. "I am something to do with Eilor. People don't know what, but they knew Eilor and knew the hate and discord he sowed in his Realm. So they assume I am something similar—something terrible, something that is hateful, or awful, and discordant." My voice broke on the last word, and I stopped, dropping my head. I wasn't sure I'd be able to keep the tears back.

"That still doesn't answer the question of whether or not Eilor is truly dead," I said, staring at the desk. "Fangorn brought it up, and I thought it was something you needed to know, to hear about. He suggested speaking with your father and brother. I've brought the message; now I must go."

I didn't wait for him to say anything. I pushed off from the desk, hearing the swish of papers that flew about in my wake. I grabbed the door handle and wrenched it open.

"Aine, wait!" I heard him say behind me. "Don't leave like this!" He caught my hand.

I wrenched my hand away from him, but he didn't let go. It forced me back toward him and without even hesitating, he pulled me to him and kissed me.

A thrill so strong ran through my body that I nearly went weak at the knees. His other arm crept around me, snugging me close to him. I let myself fall into his lips, loving the feel of him close to me.

Then I realized where I was—what I was doing. This would not do, no matter how much I liked it. I pulled myself from him, holding my hand to lips that still tingled from his.

I closed the door—all right, slammed the door as I left, not answering him at all as he called out behind me.

9

AINE

I went to my rooms, intending to go and speak to Fangorn again, after I'd calmed down. When we'd spoken earlier, I'd been focused on my family. Now, I wanted to learn more of what he knew of Eilor. It both thrilled and terrified me when we compared knowledge. Not only that, he was teaching me more on what it meant to be a dragon. I enjoyed it. Another thing I wasn't ready to share with Drake, or anyone else.

I didn't even want to think about Drake. What had he been thinking to kiss me like that? Without even so much as a by your leave!

I rubbed my lips, hoping to scrub away the memory.

If only it hadn't been so thrilling.

No. No, I couldn't think of him. I couldn't.

Dragon things. Dragon matters.

Shifting. Yes. Focus on that. Not a firm, muscled frame, and...NO! I stopped my thoughts. I won't think about it.

I hadn't managed to shift yet, but I really hadn't tried, either. Fangorn said that I might not be able to, so we were slowly working our way through lore, and the teachings. He taught me as he would one of his children.

As frightening as he could be, I didn't feel that way with him. I knew he unnerved Drake. I couldn't help that, however. This was my one remaining family member. He cared for me.

One thing Fangorn had not told me of was of his fellow captives. I'd asked about them, more than once, and he'd said, firmly, that it wasn't his story to tell. There was a secret there, and I didn't like that he was hiding it from me. I'd told him everything—outside of how I felt about the Fae royal family. Oh, all right. I could admit it to myself, at least. I'd given him my impressions of the rest of Drake's family, who just happened to be the Fae royal family. Just not my impressions of Drake. I wasn't ready to share that. Now that Drake had kissed me, I wanted to—what? Shove those feelings away even more. He wasn't for the likes of me.

I thought about the royal family for a moment. Overall, I liked them. Jharak seemed very fair. His wife, the Fae Queen, Nerida — I wasn't as sure about whether or not she was fair. In fairness to her, she was grieving the loss of her son. The fact that he was absolutely insane, and that he threatened the lives of both of her other sons, herself, and anyone else who stood in his way — that didn't seem to matter, as much as the actual loss of her son. Perhaps it was because I was not a mother. But she did seem to be wallowing it a bit much. He had tried to kill her. For me, that would've been a point that I could not have crossed. At least, in so far as making excuses for someone.

But Jharak, Jharak seemed decent. I'd heard him speaking with both of his sons on a few occasions, and I liked the kind of man he seemed to be. He was quiet and calm. Unlike his wife, he didn't seem to have any problem being glad that Cian, his eldest, was now well and truly gone. I also liked the way he spoke *to* his sons. The only parent I'd ever known was Eilor. And he was dreadful.

That left the Goblin King and Queen. Brennan and Iris. While she seemed friendlier than was normal, and it almost made my hackles rise a bit, I really liked Iris. I put my rising hackles down to the suspicion I'd been reared with.

In the short time that I had been at the Fae Castle,

and then at the Goblin Castle so that Drake could gather things he needed, and Brennan and Drake could plan a bit, Iris and I had spent a decent amount of time together. She seemed determined to be friends with me. I liked it, although I wasn't sure what one did with a friend. I never had one. There was no one, ever, in my life that I felt could be called a friend.

Well, until now. I would call Iris my friend. And her husband, Brennan. Drake's brother. He was more formal than she was, and I felt a bit more in awe of him.

Then there was Drake. While I might have my struggles with him, I very much agreed with Brennan and Jharak that he would be an excellent Dragon King. After Eilor, and all of the agendas, and machinations, a man who was open and honest was just with this kingdom needed. And Drake was open and honest. And handsome and virile and he smelled—*Stop!* I told myself. Don't think about it!

In the same vein that I felt he would be good for the Dragon Realm, I worried that like a dragon, the Dragon Realm would chew him up and spit him out.

I giggled to myself, thinking of his lists of what I called the goods and the bads. I would need to move some of those he wasn't sure of around. Later. When he wasn't so stubborn, and I didn't want to throw something at him. When I wasn't ignoring what he'd just done.

Well, perhaps I wanted to throw something at him now. Now that he'd changed everything.

Lists. Work. Focus, I told myself. Why did he have to smell like kitchens and hard work? It was intoxicating, the way his smell got around you.

Lists. Yes, think about the lists he'd showed you.

It was hard to stop thinking about the kiss or the way my lips still tingled, and my heart raced when everything else I was focusing on had Drake as a part of it. He was part of everything now.

Back to the lists.

His list wasn't a bad thing. While the list of trustworthy folk was, in fact, longer than a list of untrustworthy, the untrustworthy list was not small. One of the things that Eilor had not described his journals was whom he'd taken into his confidence here in the Dragon Realm. Initially, I didn't think he'd taken anyone into his confidence. He just was not that trusting of a man. I only knew about Niles, who was still missing, because Niles had been part of hurting me growing up. If there was a Chief Mage in this Court, Niles was it. But he'd been just as greedy and awful as Eilor, mean to me whenever he got the chance.

All in the name of "experimenting," of course.

But lately, given some of the sidelong glances, and be behind the hand remarks, I started to wonder if he did, in fact, have allies throughout the court. I knew there were people who did not wish for a king who would pay attention to the things happening in his Realm. Eilor had been so consumed with his experiments that he had left a great deal of the day to day running of the Realm to his steward and the staff that worked under his steward.

The first thing Drake had done after coming here was to meet with the steward. The next day, the steward was no longer a member of the staff.

Drake told me later that the man was stealing, billing the household for the things he stole, and did not exhibit the morale of someone who would keep a well-oiled staff running in such a large castle.

"Plus," he'd said, hands on hips with a big grin on his face, "it lets any others know that I have no problem getting rid of someone who I feel is inappropriate or disloyal. Even if it does mean my general discomfort." He laughed. "Lack of a hot meal is not a good incentive for me," he'd said through his laughter. "I've lived through eating on the road and lately, Iris' cooking."

I joined him in that laugh. The way he spoke of Iris told me that he really didn't mind her cooking.

I rubbed my lips again. Why did they continue to tingle so? I tried to keep my focus on other things.

I wasn't sure what needed to happen next, I wasn't sure of the fact that Eilor was dead, not like Brennan, and Jharak, and Drake all were. I felt that Fangorn had a good case, a good reason to be on the lookout for Eilor. A body, unfortunately, didn't prove anything.

When Drake had told me that someone thought to be a dead Eilor had been found, I had wanted to ask him if we could send out some of the members of the Castle guard to the area where the body was discovered. Maybe send along a mage. I also wanted to ask him if he had anyone he could trust. Maybe someone from the Goblin Realm? I hadn't seen many retainers that he brought with him. But then I didn't get out a lot in the castle. So perhaps he did, in fact, have some, and I was unaware. In the end, it hadn't mattered. Drake had gone to see for himself, with the other two kings. They were convinced. Were it not for Fangorn; I would be, too. But he was so sure that he should be able to leave—and he wasn't. Drake might be convinced, but I decided to be wary.

I also thought about the Dragon Realm itself. How had Eilor been able to get such a grip on the Realm? In talking with Fangorn, it seemed that his control, his ability to bend the Realm to whatever he wanted, happened very quickly. How did he manage that so efficiently? One of the things I noticed about Eilor was that while he was dogged and determined, he wasn't always efficient. He didn't always think things through logically. A lot of what he did while seemingly logical was very much based on emotion. And how he felt at the moment. I would have bet all three of his journals that Eilor had put a spell on the cages in a fit of anger. In a time when Fangorn did not give him what he wanted. And in retaliation, he made sure that Fangorn and the other dragons would never get out.

The thought of that made me almost cry again. They had to get out. They had to get out.

I wondered what Drake would do if I contacted his father. Drake was not yet formally the King of the Dragon Realm at this point, the leader of the Dragon Realm was the Fae King. So perhaps I should address my concerns to him? I knew this was a good idea in the same way that I knew it was not a good idea. It would bring my questions to the forefront while making Drake very angry. I also didn't want to talk about...The other part. When people were angry, they said all sorts of things. We didn't need to come back to what just happened.

What drove me was making sure that my dragons were never hurt. While I'd never formally met any of the rest of them, I thought of them as mine. I was the only person who knew where they were. I had put an enchantment on the door so that unless someone was me or with me, they could not open the door. I thought that perhaps they might not even see the door. But I wasn't sure.

So I wasn't sure who could actually gain access to the dragons.

Which brought me back to something I'd wanted to talk to Drake about, but...arguing. Kissing. I'd been hesitant to speak with him about this matter, so I wasn't that bothered when the anger set this aside. Fangorn was not telling me the whole truth. There was something more, something to the dragons, and why it was that we had the leaders we did. Why the Fae Realm was the center of all the Realms, and the Fae King the one who directed things. I didn't have any evidence of this. It came from comments that Fangorn dropped occasionally.

Remembering Drake's words, I wondered if they were deliberately dropped. I shook my head. I couldn't afford to doubt everything. I had to believe in something. So, even though Drake had kissed me, I still believed him a good man. Even though Fangorn might have his own agenda while sharing with me, I still believed that he cared for me, and was telling me the truth.

It seemed like, from what Fangorn had told me, whenever things went awry, particularly in the Human

Realm, it was because there was strife and arguing and sometimes even war between the races here in the Realms. What wasn't Fangorn telling me? It sat at the back of my brain, in a way that I knew there was something to this. But I couldn't get a handle on it. It was like a slippery fish that waited until the last minute to dart away from your fingers. So while I trusted both Drake and Fangorn, neither were making things any easier for me

Which brought me back to Eilor. After speaking with Fangorn, I agreed with him. I didn't think Eilor was dead. I thought that he had just gone into hiding somewhere. Drake told me that Jharak had sent their scouts everywhere. The Fae King kept a group of household guards, guards that protected him and the Queen. And anything else he deemed important enough to protect. They had found nothing. Until the body of Eilor showed up the previous night. For Jharak, apparently, that was the end of the matter.

I wished I knew what to do. I wish there were someone to advise me, someone where I didn't have to worry about their agenda. Drake wanted to be a good king and to do the right thing. To protect the Realm, to make it strong once more. In the background, Brennan and Jharak wanted the same thing. To make the Realms strong, although to not give them ideas of an uprising. I rather thought that was part of the problem.

Eilor had never fully aligned with the Fae Realm. Instead, he viewed them with a tolerant attitude of something or someone to be put up with. That attitude was also how quiet scorn began. Which was not the way to promote harmony, or have the people of your Realm see themselves as part of something bigger. So again, I wasn't sure how to handle it.

Somehow, I had to make Drake see that he should not make the assumption that Eilor was dead. That to do so would be folly, would be harmful to this realm that he was trying to bring back from the brink.

The question was how?

10

DRAKE

"Oh, for the sake of the gods," he groaned, staring at the slammed door. Maybe, maybe, if he stared long enough, she would come back. Even though they had veered in a direction that he didn't think either want to go, the gist of the conversation — that Eilor was still a threat — had not been fully addressed. He couldn't keep this from Jharak. He would need to let him know, as well as Brennan. But it felt incomplete. And he wasn't sure if that was because Aine wasn't there. That was a well he didn't wish to dip into. Not to mention he'd grabbed her, and kissed her. Where had that come from? True, it was very satisfying, and he didn't want it to end. He'd been disappointed, then horrified at himself and his actions.

Sighing, he turned around and reached into the top drawer of his desk. He pulled the small silver mirror out and held it up in front of him. "Jharak," he said. Then he waited as several moments went by.

"Yes, yes, my boy! How are you doing? Are you nearly ready? I think that we will arrive tomorrow. Will that be acceptable to you?"

Drake nodded. "That's fine, Father. I think you need to bring a few more mages, just so that Taranath has help. He's asked me if he could check for any spells daily."

Jharak nodded. "That is a good timeline," he said. "How goes the gathering of your information?"

Drake leaned on his desk, staring intently into the mirror. "That is the main reason that I have called you, Father," he said. He knew he was frowning; he couldn't help it. The news that Aine had given him was not reassuring in any fashion.

"I spoke with Aine today —"

"Has she arranged for you to see Fangorn again? So that he may look over the ring?" Jharak asked.

Drake knew his father saw her trusting him as a major stepping stone. But it had only been a month. He wasn't a worker of miracles. "No, she hasn't," he said, with some annoyance. "I've only just spoken to her about it. As for Aine—as you know, she's very protective of the dragons. She and I were...distracted by other matters.."

"Oh?"

Was that a smile he saw on Jharak's face? "Yes. But I will request a meeting today. Taranath has the ring at the moment, and perhaps he will have some answers for me as well."

"I trust that you will handle this appropriately," Jharak said.

"I know that we owe her," Drake ground out, "And I would never harm her, but she so irritating!" Drake wanted to throw up his hands. "She refuses to see any real reason! How do you talk to someone who won't see reason?" It was safer to focus on the frustrations rather than—well, than anything else.

Jharak raised one blonde eyebrow, and Drake could see his multi-colored eyes gleaming brightly. It went well with his fair skin and his blonde hair.

"I'm sure I don't know anyone like that," Jharak said dryly. "I'm sure I know no one who gets an idea into their head and refuses to hear anything different."

Drake grinned. "Yes, it is difficult living with Mother at times, isn't it?"

"You should count yourself fortunate that your mother is not within hearing," Jharak said, an answering grin on his face. "She'll portal there just to snatch you bald!" He ended with a laugh.

"Well, at least she'd be speaking to me," Drake shot back. Then he sighed. "How is she doing, Father?" He was concerned, given that his mother would be here tomorrow.

The smile didn't drop from Jharak's face, but Drake could see the weariness on his father. "She is doing less well than one would expect," he said slowly. "I had hoped that by this point in time, she would have realized that the little boy we once knew was long gone. That the man who took his place was not our son. But she has not gotten there yet, and I find I don't have the heart to berate her. I had hoped that what you are taking on would sway her--"

"I understand," Drake said slowly, "But I will tell you that I will not tolerate her hateful behavior towards myself, my future Realm, or Aine," he added, thinking about how she had been part of finishing Cian. "I can't fight Brennan's battles for him," He grinned suddenly, thinking of his brother's wife, "But I don't feel I need to. Iris does just fine."

Jharak's face broke into a smile. "She does indeed, doesn't she? I don't believe you'll need to worry about your mother. She spoke to me for a time this morning, and I believe that she will attend your ceremony and behave as you ask. I wouldn't expect much more," he ended.

Drake knew his father was torn at the way his

mother was behaving, and carrying a great deal of guilt over the matter. "If she speaks in a manner that is anything other than polite, I expect that Iris will address it immediately."

He shared a grin with Jharak. He knew that his father remembered the last time Iris "addressed" Nerida. Drake had been so impressed. Iris took no nonsense from anyone, not even the Fae Queen. She'd said all the things everyone else was thinking but hadn't wanted to say. Nerida hadn't take it well.

"How is Iris? And the child? Will the journey be safe for them?" Drake asked.

Iris was in the stage of pregnancy where there was no hiding her condition. No one would say anything, but the fears of her being mostly human were rising as the time came for the child to be born. Not to mention the idea that she was more vulnerable.

Humans didn't do well in the Fae realm. Drake was one of the few exceptions. Although it didn't happen much anymore, there were times when human children were wished away to the Goblin King. Drake was one of those children. Drake had long ago forgotten the circumstances surrounding his arrival in Fae. He could remember, when he was a boy, being angry that his human mother had wished him away. Finally, he lost his temper and yelled something about it to Brennan while they were fighting.

Brennan had taken a different point of view. He listened to Drake yell and stomp his feet and throw his toy sword, and then he'd said, in that calm, irritating manner of his, "You don't think she did you a favor?"

"A favor?" Drake had yelled. "Your own mother getting rid of you? You consider that a favor?"

Brennan had shaken his head. "No, I don't consider her wanting to be rid of you a favor. Don't be stupid, Drake. Isn't it obvious? She wished you away because she was worried something bad would happen to you there."

Drake could still remember how that felt. To hear a completely different frame of mind in regards to why his mother had sent him away. His mouth hung open, and he was unable to speak. The thoughts that raced through his mind at Brennan's words had been so big, so overwhelming, he couldn't even speak.

He hadn't been sent away because he wasn't wanted. It wasn't like the whispers he heard from the courtiers in the Fae Court. No. She sent him away to keep him safe.

Could it be possible?

That had changed everything for Drake from then on.

At that point, in his stay in the Fae Realm, it had been decided that Drake would probably live. Most human children, upon arriving in the Fae Realm did not last more than one full span of the moon. Drake had been there for six full moon cycles. Nerida asked him if he would like to call her mother. He thought about that, his heart softening as he remembered the words coming from his mother.

His mother. That moment was something that she seemed to have forgotten. That she chose him and asked that he choose her, and Jharak as well.

Damn Cian. Even after his death, Cian continued to cause problems. Listening to Brennan, Cian had always caused problems. When he finally reappeared, like a flower popping from the ground overnight, he took the whole notion of causing problems to a much greater degree.

But, Drake reflected, it had ended well. Cian is gone. Ailla is gone. Brennan and Iris are expecting a child. For himself, he did not fear for Iris. Well, he worried about her. She was a sister to him, and he wanted nothing to happen to her. Not only because he loved her, but what would it would do to his brother. He thought she would come through the birth with flying colors. No one else seemed to sure, so he kept his thoughts to himself

To his father, Drake said, "Iris continues to surprise us all, Father. I have a feeling she'll be just as strong as she has been in every other situation."

Jharak said, "I hope you're right, Drake. Your

mother and I have worried that we would never see a grandchild of our own. Neither you nor Brennan seemed all that inclined to seek out a mate. To continue your lines."

"It feels awkward to be talking about how Mother cares for her sons when she's behaving as she is," Drake said.

"I know it's tiresome," Jharak answered.

Drake could see the lines of tiredness around his father's eyes. He felt guilty adding to his worries. Well, he was going to have to feel even guiltier because there were more worries to be piled on.

"Father, she can take as long as she wants. But she'll need to keep it to herself."

Jharak smiled. "That is the sign of a man who will be a good king," he said.

Drake felt a wellspring of emotion that he hadn't felt in a long time. After so long, you didn't often hear your father say he was proud of you. But that's what Jharak just said, and it touched him.

He shook his head slightly. He was going soft.

"You don't agree?" Jharak asked.

Drake hadn't realized his head shake was visible in the mirror. "No, I'm fine. I'm just thinking of the next thing I need to talk to you about."

"That sounds ominous," Jharak said. "It seems the day for less than positive news. Go ahead, Drake."

"I spoke with Aine today, as I mentioned before we went down the path of memories, and she'd been speaking with Fangorn."

"Oh? She met with him today. Good. Is he becoming more communicative?" Jharak asked.

"I think he's very communicative. It's that Aine doesn't share everything. I am not exaggerating when I say she spends most of her days with him. And that is fine—" he held up a hand so that Jharak knew he wasn't complaining. "I have enough help to manage things, for the most part. But she seems to be unsure whether our goals are similar."

"What does he want to know?" Jharak frowned.

He sighed. "Fangorn has asked how we are sure that Eilor is dead."

"Because we saw his body, and it was very much dead." Jharak's brows furrowed.

"Well," Drake said, mentally taking the leap that he needed to contradict his father. It was still difficult, even after all this time. Then he said, "Fangorn seems to think that because of spells placed on him by Eilor, that Eilor may, in fact, be alive."

He could tell the Jharak sat up straight and held the mirror at a different angle. "What sort of spells? Why does he think the spells are still intact?"

Drake leaned back in his chair, putting his feet up on the desk. The sun warmed the room and made him feel a little bit better about this very uncomfortable conversation. While Jharak encouraged debate and discussion, he wasn't used to being told out right that he was wrong. Essentially through Aine, Drake was doing just that.

"According to Aine, Fangorn and the other dragons cannot break through the cages that form their cells. The cages are held closed via magic. Fangorn has told Aine that the cells were magically closed and locked by Eilor. And that at one point, Eilor told Fangorn that only he could break the locks free. That until he, Eilor, died, Fangorn would never get out."

He could see the Jharak leaned back in his chair. "That is a very hate-filled sort of magic," Jharak said slowly.

Drake inhaled deeply, relieved that his father didn't explode. Although why he thought Father would explode, he didn't know. Jharak rarely did. "What do you mean?"

"You know how long we live. A dragon would surely know how long a general fae lifespan is. Dragons live even longer. Eilor was telling Fangorn that he would not be free unless one of them died. That is a great deal of hate, and anger put into a spell. Do you know whether Fangorn has tried to break the spell?"

Drake nodded, holding the mirror up a little bit so

that he could sit more comfortably. "Yes. According to Aine, both she and Fangorn have attempted to break free from the cage."

Jharak tapped his finger against his lips. "Perhaps it's best that he doesn't become free just yet," he said.

Drake nodded. The room seems sharper, crisper, somehow. "That was my thought also. I happened to mention that to Aine though, and it didn't go over well."

"So what does Fangorn think would need to occur for the cells to open?" Jharak asked.

Drake noticed that Jharak wasn't addressing the idea that Eilor was alive. "Aine and I both argued today as to whether or not Eilor had to be dead, or if there just needed to be a new Dragon King on the throne. Or a combination of both. I reminded her that Eilor lied about everything, and at that point, the discussion devolved into an outright argument." He decided he didn't need to mention that he'd kissed her. No. That wasn't any concern of Jharak's.

A grin split Jharak's face. "Did she slam the door on her way out?"

Drake had to grin. "Indeed she did. Rather hard, too. I'd say she's an excellent door slammer."

Jharak laughed aloud. "That does seem to be the kind of woman we all choose," he said. "I never wanted a woman who would just say *Yes, Jharak, no, Jharak.*

Brennan might've thought he wanted a biddable wife, but we see how he ended up. And it looks like you might be the same."

Drake smiled with his father until the impact of the words hit him. "What are you talking about?" He asked. "There is nothing between me and—no! What? I think you are losing some of your reason!" He couldn't believe that Jharak thought—no. He was interested in no one, certainly not Aine! The kiss—it was merely a moment of stress, an expression of the intensity of the moment.

Jharak's grin got wider if that was possible. Right in front of him. He didn't even try to hide his amusement. "You don't think so, son? Allow me to know my offspring. And allow me to have a slightly greater experience with women that you, my son."

"Don't let mother hear you say such things," Drake said frostily, unable to believe that they were having this conversation. Weren't they discussing the blasted Eilor? How in the hell did Aine and what Drake thought of her come into this?

"It is important that you now start thinking of your line, and the legacy you will leave after you are gone. You are going to be the king," Jharak said, and Drake could see that the grin had faded a little bit. Which meant that for now, Jharak was, in part, serious.

"Father, I don't want to talk about such things. We

need to focus on the question of whether or not Eilor is dead. I was with you. I saw his body. It was him." Then he sighed. "I hate to admit it, but Aine's questions have made me think. Fangorn has experienced Eilor in his magic for far longer than we did. He knows Eilor in a way that we never did. Eilor hid that from us."

Jharak looked like he wanted to say something non-Eilor related, but he must have decided to keep it to matters of the Realm as he only said, "Your logic is sound, but I'm not sure I can agree with you. However, please know that I take your comments into consideration. So in addition to everything else that you are doing, you will need to keep an eye out."

Drake threw up his hands, the papers scattering with the wind of his movement. "With what time, Father? Do you know how busy I am? I can't keep everything straight!"

"Then you'll need to find some courtiers to help you with the planning. That is what they are there for. To be helpful. Not just take up space and eat the food." Jharak said mildly. "I'm not entirely sure I see the concern, Drake."

"You don't see the concern? How do we know who to trust? I know that I can trust you, and Brennan and I can even trust that damned Aine, but how else do I know to trust people? How do I know that all of the people in this court were not in league with Eilor somehow? I don't wish to end up dead in my bed!"

"You never know that any courtier is truly loyal," Jharak said, refusing to respond to Drake's anger. "All you can do is choose the person you think is best, and then you hope that you have not made a mistake. That's part of being the king, Drake."

"Yet another reason why I really didn't want this," mumbled Drake.

"That part of the discussion is long past," said Jharak briskly.

"Perhaps for you, since you're not here having to wade through this mess!" Ground out Drake.

"Consider it the best training possible," Jharak said, the grin, returning to his face ever so slightly. "As well you know, the best way to learn is by getting right into it."

Drake resisted the urge to roll his eyes. His father had just quoted his own words about swordplay right back to him. It was aggravating to be on the losing end of a discussion with Jharak. Particularly when he beat you with your own words.

"Stick with it, Drake," Jharak said. "While there may be those with agendas not in line with your own, I would bet that there are plenty in that court who are happy that Eilor is gone. Fearful, unsure of whether to commit their support you, but happy that he is gone.

From all that Aine has told us, I don't think he was a good king. Let me give you a little advice. One way that you can win those who are hesitant or even scornful to you is to establish the rhythm of daily life."

"What you talking about?" Drake asked.

"Make sure they have enough to eat. Make sure that the marketplace is full. Make sure that if someone wishes to buy their daughter a new dress, or their son a sword, that the merchants are there, and able to bring their wares for show. Put things into the hands of those who want them. Put a coin or two into the pockets of those selling." Jharak laughed at Drake's expression.

Drake knew he must look like a fool, staring as he did at his father's words. "I don't understand. The market will help me be a better king?"

"Quit worrying about the bigger problems. Focus on the smaller problems. And pick one courtier, one that you feel is relatively trustworthy, and ask him or her about the marketplace. About where could you go to find certain items that they might need for the coronation? You would be surprised at what people tell you when they think you're just asking about the daily things. Take note. And," he added, frowning slightly. "I would not have Aine with you when you did this."

"Why not?" Drake asked. He knew that Jharak trusted Aine, so this was unexpected advice.

"From what Aine has said, who she is, and what

people think of her, or think they know—courtiers may not be as willing to speak freely in front of her. I don't know this, of course. I am merely going on the things both you and Aine have told me."

Drake interrupted, "Aine said the very thing to me today!"

Jharak nodded, and continued, "This way, it allows the people of the court to see that you mean to rule on your own. That whatever else may be going on with Aine, your role as the King will not be dependent on having her as someone who's close to you. At least," Jharak smiled broadly, "not yet."

Drake ignored his father's blatant innuendo. If Jharak wanted to believe that, more power to him. He would not give such notions any further notice. If you encouraged Jharak, he only got worse. "That's a good idea to just focus on one or two courtiers at a time, asking about this or that." He considered which ones he could find today.

"I have been known to have those once in a while," Jharak said dryly.

"Well, I'm very glad that I was here to witness it," Drake snapped back.

Jharak laughed. "I hope that helps you some, Drake. I hope that picks you up a bit so that you are not moping about like a spoiled child,"

"I have never been a spoiled child!" Drake said.

Jharak only laughed "I'll give you regards to your mother, whether you do or not, and whether she wants it or not," he said. "Now go find yourself a courtier who needs a dress." The mirror winked out.

Drake leaned back a little further, enjoying the sunlight on his face from the window. The sun remained one of the reasons that he kept this room. He thought about what his father said. Why hadn't he thought of asking those who lived here?

Because he never had to think about it before. When he lived with Brennan, it had always been taken care of. He'd never sat in with Brennan and his steward, preferring the tiltyard.

He sighed. Perhaps he would need to call Brennan and ask to borrow his steward. Since he'd dismissed the man who claimed to be a steward here. The only thing that man had been was a thief.

He wasn't sure though, how the Dragon Court would look at having an actual member of the Goblin Court, who was also a goblin, here in the court. Brennan's steward was half goblin, half fae. He sighed again. He would need to ask Aine.

Who, if he was correct, wasn't speaking to him right now.

11

AINE

I paced in my room, not sure what to do next. I wished I had was someone to talk to. I had one of the mirrors that all the members of the royal family had. They could call each other, at any time. No need to send a message, or messenger. I was frustrated with my inability to make Drake see that this really was a legitimate concern—that the dragons may not be able to be free. That Eilor may not actually be dead.

As I paced back and forth, my thoughts got me nowhere. That's not entirely true. They did give me somewhere. To the conclusion that I didn't want to reach.

I was going to have to take Drake to see Fangorn again. I would probably need to show him the door. I had meant to ask only to bring the ring, but I would probably need to bring Drake as well. He wasn't going to let me just traipse off with the ring of the Dragon King.

Which meant I would need to talk to him and be pleasant. Both things I didn't want to do at the moment.

I didn't think that Fangorn would be upset. He had said to me that he felt it was probably time he started to speak at length to the Fae royal family. When I expressed to him that I was worried about exposing him and the rest of the dragons to the fae that had killed them, he said, "That is a long time in the past. I am not the same dragon I once was. And I would doubt that Jharak is the same king that he was at the time. Furthermore, Eilor is not in power any longer. I truly believe he was one of the driving forces behind how things ended up."

So what was it that held me back? The fact that Drake had kissed me? Or that I wouldn't be upset if it happened again?

I drew back from my thoughts. That was not the direction I wanted them to go.

I sat on the bed, rubbing my face with my hands. This room, although beautiful, seemed almost too fancy for me. In all my years growing up with Eilor, I had always slept on a pallet in one of the small rooms off of his room. As I'd gotten older, I'd been concerned that he might have less than honorable intentions towards me — as though his intentions towards me were ever honorable— but he never bothered me. For which I thanked the stars. Had he come near me, I would've killed him. And while I was not the happiest person, I didn't wish to die.

I looked down at myself, surprised, as always, to see the latest fine gown that I wore. I'd needed to change the lovely purple gown. Somehow, it had torn. Probably Drake's fault, I thought snidely. I was content to assign fault for all things to him at this point.

Although in regards to my clothing, I ended up changing far more often than I had when breeches were my preferred manner of garb. The current gown was set in tones of green and blue that contrasted nicely with my darker hair. My eyes were also blue-green, something that Fangorn had noted. He told me that my eyes would probably go very green when I was angry or experiencing some other strong emotion. That it would be the dragon in me coming out. I had spent so long keeping my emotions muted, to survive. I couldn't imagine just letting my emotions show as I felt them.

That made me think of the next thing in our lessons. I'd not told Drake, but much of the time I spent with Fangorn was spent learning. He and I had been going through the histories, with Fangorn letting me know what my family was on the dragon side of things. He couldn't tell me much of anything about Lionel's wife Maria when he'd shared memories of my father. He remembered Lionel's mother. He said she had been a sweet girl, and that she hadn't been afraid of him in either his fae or dragon form. Initially, he'd been gentle with her, and they grown to care for each other. His eyes gleamed brightly as he spoke of her, so I figured he was telling me the truth.

In evaluating myself, I didn't look horrible; I didn't look like a dragon. But Fangorn told me, in spite of my diluted dragon blood that I might be able to shift. If I couldn't shift, I would still have some of the powers of the dragons.

"Your dragon blood will not be silenced," he said to me.

If I was honest with myself, and at this point, I needed to, that's what kept me from bringing Drake down to meet Fangorn again. Forget about Jharak or Brennan — Drake would be bad enough. Then he would see all the horrible things that had come together to make me. My relatives were captive beasts, kept caged because they were dangerous.

I looked at my dress again. I was well-dressed, thanks to Iris. A true fae lady.

But I wasn't. I was the furthest thing from it. I got

up, determined to take action while my courage was high. I sighed. This would probably mean I needed to apologize. I so hated doing this with Drake. He never let an apology just sit. There had to be a few digs throughout the rest of the day, just to let you know that he knew he was right. He could be so annoying sometimes. All that was before the matter of kissing came into it.

I went to the mirror and checked my hair. I looked over my dress and saw no signs of crying or any sort of stains. I looked around the room once more. If you didn't know any better, I looked like I was just another fae courtier, on my way to an audience with the king.

If only...

I inhaled deeply, drew back my shoulders, and open the door. Time to go beard the dragon in his den and beg for forgiveness. Well, sort of.

I told Drake one time that it was very fitting that the Dragon Real would have a king named Drake. He had not been amused. As I moved down the hallway heading towards the main rooms of the castle, I debated how I would start. It's sort of hard to reenter conversation with dignity when you've slammed your way out of it previously.

I was so intent on figuring out the right words; I didn't see him coming towards me. At least, not until I ran right into him.

"Oh I am so — oh, it's you," I said crossly. "You need to look where you're going."

Drake scowled, rubbing his shoulder were my head hit him. "I could safely say the same, ladyship," he growled.

"What do you want?" I asked, forgetting for a moment that I was actually going to see him.

"I was coming to talk with you," he began.

Then I remembered I'd been doing the same. With the plan of apologizing. Here I was being angry, again.

"What are you doing?" He asked.

"I was actually coming to see you," I said.

"Really, why is that?" He looked slightly suspicious.

I searched his face carefully. There is not a trace of smugness on it, but I felt that it was close behind.

"I would rather not discuss it out here in the corridor," I said. "Will you walk with me? I have something that you need to see."

Drake's eyebrows went up to his hairline. He looked like he badly wanted to say something, and I realized too late that my words could be taken in a number of different ways. Not exactly the footing I wanted to get off with on him. "Don't be stupid," I snapped. "I really don't want to discuss this out in the open. Now, are you coming with me or not?" I turned around, noting that it was hard to look dignified when one skirts twirled around one.

"Oh, I wouldn't miss this for anything, ladyship," he said, falling in step beside me.

I thought this was the right decision. I needed to show him the door, let him see how to get to the dragons, and alter the spell so that he could go on his own. It was the right choice. I'd blindfolded him before, so that he couldn't find it again.

Or so I told myself. I wasn't sure this was going to go well at all. What if he recoiled in disgust at me, once I laid out all my concerns? If he showed me any sort of negative emotion, it would crush me. He was the first person that I'd trusted to let him see parts of the real me. Letting him see Fangorn like this would be exposing all of me. Especially as Fangorn would be able to read me like a book. I hope it wasn't making a mistake.

We reached the small hallway that led to Eilor's former rooms. There was a door that was kept locked when Eilor was here, and I'd continued locking it. I didn't want anyone stumbling upon the dragons.

"Where are we going? I haven't been here before," Drake asked, looking around him.

"I found this by accident. I was looking for the rooms that..." I hesitated. Then I took a breath and continued. "That Eilor had said my mother was in when she got away. This hallway," I said, unlocking the door with a key I kept on my person, "Led to his rooms.

He put her close to him so that he could keep watch on her, and keep her from the rest of the castle."

I could feel my heart beating more quickly than usual, thudding against the walls of my chest. I could hear the *whoosh-whoosh* of my heightened heartbeat in my ears. I took a deep breath, deciding the best thing to do was just to get it all out. "I am taking you to the doorway that leads to the caverns. To get there, you will need to access this corridor." I held the door open, allowing him to enter.

"The doorway leads directly to the caverns where the dragons are caged. I've gone over it in my head, and I can't see any other way out. You need to be able to access Fangorn without me. I would prefer you didn't, but you are the king of this Realm. I believe this is the appropriate thing to do. The other dragons are not awake, as you know. I'm not even sure that they will wake up. Fangorn told me that they've been asleep for so long. He's afraid they have become frozen in some manner." I turned to lock the door behind me and then tucked the key away. I'd need to have one made for Drake. Then I turned around to find him watching me. "But it's time for you to meet Fangorn as the king. Not merely as the man I am bringing to him. You might want to bring the dragon ring you took from Eilor, too. I mentioned it to Fangorn, and he asked to see it."

His mouth dropped open, and I could tell this was

not what he was expecting. He recovered quickly. "Really? I'm surprised, Aine. I didn't expect you to trust me with your dragons alone. But I am very pleased and much honored that you choose to do so."

Such a formal and grateful speech from him. That was not what I had been expecting either. And I liked how it sounded when he called them my dragons. Perhaps that would be a way for me to make a place for myself. As the guardian for the dragons. Making sure they were never used again, never harmed again, and never made to suffer as Fangorn and the rest of them had for thousands of years.

"Let me call Taranath," he said. He stepped away, and I heard him speaking. Then he turned back to me, and said, "Taranath is bringing it here. I asked him to portal, as I don't wish to waste time."

At his words, a light flared in the hallway. I hadn't planned on this—another person knowing where the door was located! But—it was Taranath. He would not harm them.

"My lord, my lady," Taranath stepped out. "I have brought the ring. I can find no reason why it would have shocked the Fae King. If it hasn't shocked or harmed you, I think you are safe to handle it." He held out the ring to Drake, who took it.

"Thank you," said Drake. "Now go. We're on an errand we cannot speak of at the moment."

Taranath must be used to this, because he bowed, and walked right back through the still-open portal. Then it winked out as if it were never there.

"Well, we waiting for? Can we go now?" Once the idea was in his head, Drake would not be deterred.

I smiled. "Yes, we can go now. Be prepared. It's a long set of stairs, as you may recall."

I walked on, looking for the torch that was positioned above the door. I was trusting Drake, but I felt more comfortable being trusting in small steps. I'd see how he did with this step before I allowed him full access without me there. Once we got the torch, I stopped and said the spell to open the door.

Drake noted all this, I could tell, but didn't say anything. He followed me as I walked into the stairway and then as we went down the stairs a few steps, the door closed behind us. I started the descent, and torches on the wall lit as we moved near them, lighting the way. It was a good thing. You could fall and kill yourself on this stairway otherwise.

"This is amazing! Did you do this with your magic?"

I shook my head, even though I knew he couldn't see me. "No, it was like this when I first came down here. I don't know if Eilor did it, or if someone else did. The Dragon Castle is very old. Fangorn tells me it's been here for as long as he can remember and he is at least six thousand years old."

There was silence behind me for a moment, and then Drake spoke. "I did not realize that he was so old. Are all the dragons as old as he is?"

"I don't think so. We haven't talked about that much, that I get the impression that he's one of the older dragons still alive."

I heard a slight shushing as Drake ran his hands along the wall. "This is well-built. There's no dampness along the stones. It doesn't smell musty, or ill-used."

"Every time I go into the cavern, I am amazed," I said. "I don't know how Eilor got the dragons in here. I don't know how anyone got the dragons in here. They're huge. And this is all underneath the castle. I don't know how they were brought in." It made me sad to think of sleeping away the years, trapped.

I understood Drake's concern about letting them roam free because all the dragons in here were enormous. And I didn't know those who were sleeping —the other ten dragons. There were six males and four females. According to Fangorn, these were also members of my family. Not directly, I thought. At least, that was how I interpreted his comments. But family aside, who knew what they would do? Who knew how they would behave? There were no records of why these eleven dragons were chosen, and all the rest of the dragons died or were put to death. Fangorn himself could not tell me much about it other than he was surprised that he was chosen as a dragon who would go on. He had said they disagreed with the war, but I got the impression they had not done a great deal to stop it.

In spite of all that, they were the last members of part of who I was. No matter what, I couldn't ignore that. I didn't want to although the thought of being part of those massive beings scared me a little.

I felt Drake bump into me as he stepped oddly on the step behind me. His hands went out—one to the wall, and one to my hand. His skin felt warm—really warm. A quick squeeze, and then his touch disappeared.

I was pleased that he was behind me and couldn't see the blush I knew stained my cheeks. The heat on my face told me that his touch sent the blood right to my face.

Why did his touch have this effect on me? Why now, when I had so many other concerns to grapple with?

Why did I like the feel of his hand, his warm skin, on mine? I shook my head to clear it and put the feel of his skin and everything else out of my head. I didn't have time for this.

Drake and I didn't speak for the rest of the descent.

As we reach the bottom, I stopped on a step, and put my hand out towards them. "I need to ask you if you can allow me to take the lead on this? Fangorn knows me. In so far as he can, I think he trusts me. He will be accepting of you if I can show him that I trust you. We discussed the ring, but I didn't suggest I bring you with it. No matter how you feel...About me," I stumbled a little. *Don't blush, don't blush!* I told myself furiously. "And that you will not behave in a way that I do not wish." That should cover any inappropriate behavior.

"I won't do anything that you don't want me to," Drake said. I could tell by his tone that he meant it. There was not an ounce of laughter in his words. In the dim light of the staircase, since we were between two torches, he reached over and placed a hand on my arm.

"I know that this is a big step for you to trust me. I'm not going to harm your dragons. If you can assure me that your dragons will not harm me or any of the other fae, I can give you the same assurances."

He had not been this honest with me before. Frankly, I hadn't thought about why he would be so concerned. I was too busy worrying about what happened to the dragons — my dragons. I couldn't think of them like that though. Even as much as it thrilled me to think of myself as one of them.

"They are not my dragons, Drake," I said. "They are no one's dragons. Such thinking is what landed them where they are, and allowed for Eilor to abuse them. I prefer to be thought of as a guardian for them, making sure that things between the dragons and the fae go smoothly. But they are not mine." I didn't mean to rebuke him, but I felt very strongly about that. Even though I called them mine to myself—no one else would own them. Not even me.

He laughed a little. That made me glad to see, to know that I hadn't offended him.

"All right, ladyship. Take me to the dragons. I promise not to annoy or anger the guardian. I didn't last time, so I should be able to manage this time as well."

From the tone of his voice, I could tell that was all I was going to get as far as assurances. It would have to do. The rest would be up to me, and Fangorn. And eventually, hopefully, the rest of the dragons.

As we reach the last step of the staircase, I turned to him again. "It's going to be a bit of a shock, seeing how large this is, and knowing that it's underneath the castle."

As we walked out into the cavern, he slowed behind me. When I looked at him, he was looking up at the ceiling and all around. The cavern itself was in the shape of a horseshoe, and it had cages all around it.

There were five on each side of the horseshoe and one in the center. On the right side of the half-circle, it looked as though there was no dragon in the second cage from the center. All the rest of the cages had a slumbering dragon visible. I'd kept the blindfold on him before until we reached the cage, and told Fangorn to keep the torches dim.

I didn't bother with that now. I wanted him to see everything.

The one that looked empty was Fangorn's cage, and I walked straight to it. I could feel Drake beside me, restraining himself, but ready--and the sense of who he was as a warrior washed over me. It was almost as though he could turn it on and off like one would light a candle and then blow it out. He had definitely lit the warrior flame.

Just as I was thinking about what to say, I heard the deep voice of Fangorn's rumble from his cage.

"So...no longer merely the son of the Fae King. But the new Dragon King--and the ring, here to see me," he said.

At that moment, I remembered all that I'd heard about dragons before meeting Fangorn. They were crafty, sly; they could be incredibly manipulative. And they were smart. Very smart. With that one sentence and the timbre of his voice, Fangorn made sure that we both knew we were dealing with a dragon.

And as quickly as it came, the strangeness of this Fangorn before me vanished. I knew that he was setting the tone, trying to make sure that he didn't lose more than he already had. I knew the weaknesses; I knew where the armor had chinks in it.

I understood. My heart swelled with love—love—for this father of mine. When had that happened? Today was a jumble of all the things I'd not expected.

With probably more mind reading than I cared for, I felt a rush of—something—from Fangorn. He knew how I was feeling. For the moment, I was glad.

I cleared my throat and got to the business that brought us here.

"My lord Fangorn, you remember Lord Drake? You are correct; he is soon to be the king of the Dragon Realm."

Fangorn unfurled himself in the corner where he sat, standing to his full height. While he was in fae form, he was all dragon. The dragon was visible behind the man. The torch nearest his cage glowed more brightly as we came closer, and I could see the gleam of his eyes in the torchlight.

I waved my hand around, having learned from previous visits that that would make the torches shine more brightly. Next to me, I felt a little start as Drake jerked a bit. It was a shock, seeing just how tall Fangorn was.

My grandfather, I thought. I couldn't suppress the pride that made me feel.

Then I noticed how Drake and Fangorn were staring at each other. Oh dear. I needed to sort this immediately.

"Grandfather, it has taken a great deal for me to allow Drake to come with me today. Just as it has taken a great deal for him to come, and trust my judgment. I would ask that you both trust me, and see if we can't find a solution to the dilemma we find ourselves in."

I never called him grandfather before. I'd referred to him as my grandfather, even in front of him a few times. But I never actually addressed him as such. There was a silence as both of them digested what it was I had just said.

"Lord Fangorn," Drake began, "I appreciate that you are willing to see me once more. Aine tells me you have offered help with the ring and whether Eilor is truly dead. I appreciate it. The former King of the Dragon Realm has served poorly as your guardian. Your granddaughter has told me some of what you have endured, and I am sorry."

"That means something, coming from the fae," rumbled Fangorn. "But not all fae are like Eilor. At one time, I might have said differently. However, after a millennia or two in a cage, with only Eilor to look at, I have accepted that my shortsightedness was in part what put me here."

As I watched, Drake smiled, and it looked to be

genuine. "While I do not have your years, My lord, I am learning all the time that the things I did when I was young are lucky that in that they allowed me to live."

The merest hint of a smile quirked up the corner of one side of Fangorn's mouth. He was not given to a great deal of expression. I always imagined it was because he couldn't afford to show any sort of expression around Eilor. I understood that intimately. But I could feel it, feel it in my bones, that he was pleased. That he felt that there was hope.

I knew he felt it because I felt it too.

12

DRAKE

*H*e couldn't believe that she'd actually brought him down here. He couldn't believe that without a huge fight she had allowed him to see her dragon sire. To see all of the dragons. She'd hidden them all before. He'd only had a glimpse of the dragon before him. A sense more than anything. It made him wonder if Aine and Fangorn had placed some sort of mist, or spell, over everything other than what they wanted him to see. The thought angered him briefly, and then it passed. It didn't matter. She was trying to save the dragons.

Drake found her thought process regarding them interesting. That she did not wish for him to call them her dragons. Because ownership had gotten them into trouble in the first place. The dragon shifter didn't look quite as ferocious as he had when he'd first approached the bars of the cage.

Drake decided that he would take the same manner he'd always taken, one of direct honesty. It served him well before, and while dragons had a reputation for being shifty, there was no sense in attempting to lie.

"How did you come to be here?" He asked Fangorn.

"I don't know," Fangorn said simply. "Once the war had ended, and the peace treaty had been executed, along with most of my brethren, we," he waved his arm to encompass all the dragons in the cavern, "Were told that we'd been selected to live. For myself, with my mates and my children gone, I didn't see the sense. But I was given no choice. All the fae mages came together, and they began to exercise a spell. That's the last thing I remember until I woke up here. My best guess?" He grinned, but it was a grin of cynicism. "That it was done by magic somehow. Who could lift a dragon?" He snorted at his humor.

Then Fangorn continued, "The Dragon Castle has been here for as long as I could remember. We preferred the mountains, only coming here to communicate with the subjects of the Dragon Realm who were something other than dragons. They did exist," he said, giving Drake a hard look.

Drake fought the urge to grimace. His disbelief

must have shown on his face. He'd need to be careful. Fangorn was extremely perceptive. Probably more so, given this circumstances. He arranged his face in what was hopefully a neutral, encouraging expression.

After a moment, Fangorn continued. "Perhaps this was here before. I don't know. Dragons did not live in the castle before the war. Maybe it one time they did." Fangorn shrugged his shoulders.

"Do you generally sleep? When was the last time all of you awake?" Drake asked.

I have been awake since the birth of my son Lionel," Fangorn said. "Ever since he escaped, Eilor kept me awake. In case Lionel had tried to contact me somehow. And after Lionel's death, he would not allow me to go back into a slumber." The hatred and bitterness seeped into his tone.

Drake couldn't blame him. Aine had told him of her parents, and she'd been visibly shaken as she related the story. He couldn't imagine the horror of knowing that you had yet another child and that this child had finally lived to maturity, only to lose him again. And then discover that your sworn enemy had killed him, and the most horrific way possible. Well, Drake didn't know if it was horrific. But given that this was Eilor...well, it hadn't been pleasant.

He decided, rather than to reminisce about history, ask about the current problem in hand. "Aine tells me you don't believe Eilor is dead. Can you tell me why? I don't think I completely understood what she was trying to tell me. I also know that I have seen the body of the fae I knew as Eilor, and I removed this," He held up the ring, glancing out of the side of his eyes at Aine, wanting her to know that he didn't blame her. And that he took the blame on himself for his lack of understanding.

Fangorn smiled, and in that smile, Drake could see where the dragons were so feared. While Fangorn was a fae man at the moment, and he was smiling, the dragon was just beneath the surface. Aine had told him Fangorn was a large blue dragon, and his eyes were a bright green. She also mentioned that when he was in high emotion, his eyes glowed green as a Fae man.

They were glowing green right now.

Fangorn spoke slowly, carefully. It appeared he was attempting to choose his words with care. Drake got the sense Fangorn wanted to be sure he was understood, rather than choose words with which to manipulate.

"At one point, after Lionel had escaped, and before Lionel and Maria were found and brought back here, Eilor told me in a fit of anger that I would never be free."

Drake could hear the finality of the idea of forever

in those words. He felt very young in comparison to the being in front of him. This was also exactly what Aine had told him.

Fangorn continued, "He also chose to share that he had overseen placing us in these cages. That he had been declared the Dragon King before we were ever brought here, and that as such, he had utilized his magic as the Dragon King to ensure we would never be free."

An ancient deep anger rolled through the cavern with Fangorn's words. The torches on the walls flickered as though a wind whirled about the ceiling. Drake watched the movement around them. It was in stark contrast with the stillness of the fae shifter before him.

Fangorn continued. "He told me that the only way these bars would be removed would be if he were no longer the Dragon King. At the time, I thought that meant when he died. As dragons generally can outlive fae, I was certain that at some point, I would be free again. But after he told me, after keeping it secret for so long, he dropped hints. Almost as though he were taunting me."

Fangorn inhaled deeply, and abruptly turned and walked away from the bars of the cage. Drake started to speak but stopped when he felt the pressure of Aine's hand on his arm. Her touch was like a live flame to his hand. He closed his mouth and waited.

Eventually, Fangorn walked back towards the bars of the cage. His eyes were like torches themselves. Green, angry torches.

"The impression I got from him, although I cannot say if it was correct, was that until another sat on the throne, I would never be free. I also got the impression that he would need to die. I understand that impressions are not fact and that my impressions are colored by my hatred of Eilor. I would in fact like to see him dead before me. Preferably in pieces," Fangorn finished, as though he were asking for another slice of cake.

"I believe," Drake said, "that you will have to — what is it that Iris, the new Goblin Queen, says? Get in line."

Fangorn stared at him for a moment, and then he burst out laughing. It was the oddest sound. It was deep; deep enough to make your bones shudder. It echoed around the cavern, and the torches glowed brighter. Unlike before with the level of anger, now the torches glowed as brightly as the dragon's eyes. The cavern felt warmer, and not quite as foreboding or crushing.

When Fangorn had stopped laughing, the traces of

the smile lingered on his face. "Who is Iris, and why is the fact that she is the Goblin Queen significant?"

"Iris is part human, a human girl that Brennan – that's the Goblin King — and I found when we accidentally landed into the Human Realm. She is now the Goblin Queen."

"I thought humans did not survive in the Fae Realm," Fangorn said.

"Initially, I was human also," Drake said. "You are right. Most humans do not. Iris and I are the exceptions."

"You were once human?" Fangorn came closer to the bars, peering out. "You don't look human at all. Of course," he added, "Neither does Aine, and her mother was a full human if Eilor's journal is to be believed."

"You think that he lied in the journal?" Drake asked. He considered it, but he thought maybe he was a little too pessimistic. "I would think that the journal will be the one place he kept more accurate recordings of everything that happened."

Incredibly, Aine rolled her eyes. "We have been over this more than once, Fangorn. I don't think he lied in the journals. I think the journals for the one place he did tell the truth. Probably the only place he ever told the truth."

Drake was struck at the level of anger in her voice. Clearly, she and Fangorn had been doing a lot of talking. He wondered just how much. How much time did she spend down here? He didn't notice a massive difference in her. Would he? She was so secretive about the dragon side of her.

"So do you believe that Eilor still alive? We found a body," Drake said. He wanted to keep this meeting – or whatever it was – on track. There were too many other unanswered questions that got in the way otherwise.

"Where did you find the body?" Fangorn asked

Drake noticed that Fangorn and Aine had the same quiet, deliberate way of speaking. As though they didn't need to raise their voice, or seek attention because the simple fact of the way they spoke brought it right to them. As though they didn't feel the need to shout ever, because why would they? When they spoke, people would listen.

"I found it with my brother Brennan and my father, Jharak. It was found when guards were patrolling the outer edges of the Fae Realm, at least, the area around the Fae Castle." He felt the need to be specific, as the entire set of Realms was called the Fae Realm. He also hoped that Fangorn would forget the Jharak was one of the people to put him here.

No such luck.

"Jharak? Jharak is still alive? Interesting. Aine mentioned that, but I wasn't sure she had it correct.

Has he expressed an interest in coming to see us? Those who he locked away so many years ago?"

"Yes, as a matter of fact, he has," Drake answered. "I believe, like you, he has seen the error of decisions made when he was younger. Like you, I believe he would like a chance to do things differently."

Aine looked at him with what he would almost call a grateful expression. If he thought she would shoot a grateful expression his way. And not just shoot him, preferably with a bow and arrow. At close range. Or perhaps she was not as angry as she had been with him. He hoped this was the case. He didn't like fighting with her. He would rather—he stopped that thought immediately.

His thoughts were interrupted by Fangorn clearing his throat.

"I'm sorry, I was just following our train of thought," Drake said, to cover his lapse into thinking of Aine yet again. "Did you ask me something?"

He was sure he saw Fangorn hide a smile. Was he a mind reader? Damn the man – or the dragon – whatever he was.

"I asked you if you thought that several thousand years of imprisonment could be made up by good intentions," Fangorn said.

Drake wasn't expecting that sort of response. And here he thought the dragon was ready to make peace.

"Well, I suppose he would want to know if you thought that several thousand years imprisonment was enough to make up for all the lives lost when the war broke out," he replied. Drake braced himself to move back should Fangorn try to claw at him or something similarly dragon-like.

Instead, Fangorn smiled and crossed his arms. "That is a wiser answer than you probably thought, son of Jharak."

He'd forgotten how good it felt to be a son of Jharak. He'd been Drake of the Goblin Realm for so long, that Drake, son of Jharak felt odd. But good.

Fangorn, however, had moved on to something different. "Who was the man I saw with the daughter of Eilor?"

Aine spoke up at this point. "That was Cian, son of Jharak."

Fangorn frowned. "I thought the Jharak only had two sons," he said. The torches dimmed as his brows came closer together. Drake wondered how he did it.

"I am surprised that Eilor did not share this with you," Drake said. "But it's no great secret. Cian sustained an injury as a child. He was taken away to recuperate, and the castle where he was taken to broke out in a fire was destroyed. Cian was assumed dead. Somehow, we're not quite sure how, he ended up here, in the Dragon Realm. So while he is—was—my father's son, Eilor is the one who raised him."

At this point, Fangorn interrupted. "He was not sane, that man. I did not think Eilor was sane either, but Cian came to his madness via a different, darker route."

"Well, no one knew what a threat he was, until recently. However, he is no longer a threat," Drake said, his voice ringing with satisfaction. He still felt no pity for the man that he had helped to kill. Cian would have killed them all. Without an ounce of remorse. He was like a wild animal, foaming at the mouth. Such men — and animals — could not be allowed to live.

"Oh? He is dead then?" Fangorn asked.

Drake nodded, "Yes, he is dead. A month past."

Fangorn looked at Aine then. "This must please you, daughter," he said.

"Yes, it does. However, Fangorn, I would be much happier if we knew for sure that Eilor was gone."

"But we don't know that he's alive!" Drake said, in some frustration. "We're going round and round here, but you're not giving me any reason as to why he might be alive. You bring up the spell and the fact that you are not free. But that is not based on hard fact, only supposition. I have seen a body, with my own eyes! I have taken the ring of the Dragon King, a ring Eilor prized and was never seen without! I need to understand why you don't believe a dead body!" He tried to keep his temper, but he wasn't getting anything that would count as an answer. And to bring this to Jharak, or Brennan—he needed to have a more concrete answer.

"Do you believe you could break the spell?" Fangorn asked.

Drake shrugged. "I'm not the magician. I am skilled in magic, yes. But it is not my specialty. I could, if you were amiable, bring in the mage of my brother Brennan. He is exceptionally skilled."

Fangorn and Aine exchanged a glance that said much, although Drake couldn't tell exactly what. He wasn't sure he liked her being so close to the elder dragon. Dragons were notoriously self-absorbed, although being a prisoner for so long seemed to have altered Fangorn somewhat. He also seemed to care very much for Aine.

But were all of the things Fangorn seemed to think or feel enough to trust him? Drake wasn't sure.

"I would be pleased to meet the mage of your brother," Fangorn said formally. "I will be honest with you, son of Jharak; I am not ready to see your father. Nor am I ready to see your brother. I am unsure that I could keep my temper. Even after all this time." He held up a hand. "I know, my reasoning is not very fair. But I want to be honest. I don't wish to die in this cage.

I would like to be free, to fly again," he stopped speaking for a moment, and Drake could see the sheer longing on his face.

"I would like to see my brethren go free once more, although I'm not sure if that's possible."

"Why were the rest of them chosen along with you? Why were the lot of you allowed to live?" Jharak had never discussed this with him. Perhaps some insight from the dragon side of things would help to determine their fate, Drake thought.

"Because the eleven of us openly tried to stem the great war," Fangorn said quietly. "None of us supported it. All the rest of the dragons did. While there were not as many dragons as there are fae, there were enough of us. Enough who created a threat, and did what they could to take over the Realms. At the time," he looked off into the distance and Drake could tell he saw something long in the past, "I thought we were fortunate to be allowed to live. Now," he looked down. And then back up at Drake, and his eyes blazed bright green, "I am not so sure."

"I will be happy to contact Brennan's mage, and arrange for him to come and visit with you. In the meantime, what can I do to make things easier?" Drake found that he liked Fangorn, much more than he thought he would. He wasn't sure that he trusted him, nor that he trusted him or his intentions in regards to

Aine. But the man was brave, both as a dragon and as a fae. He did not shrink from his own actions, nor did he make apologies or excuses. That was the mark of a warrior, and Drake could respect that.

He could swear that he saw the surprise on the dragon's face. "You cannot set me free, but I would appreciate," he thought for a moment. "I would appreciate fresh meat."

Drake looked at Aine. "He doesn't get fresh meat?"

She shook her head. "No. Eilor never wanted to alert the kitchens. So he fed them only salted meat, meat that those in kitchens wouldn't notice missing."

"That would be misery," Drake said directly to Fangorn. "Do you have a favorite meal?"

"Sheep, or cattle," Fangorn said. He didn't sound like he believed Drake would make it happen.

That was all right, Drake thought. He could understand the skepticism. "I will do my best, Lord Fangorn," he said with a slight bow of his head.

13

AINE

I couldn't believe how happy it made me that Drake and Fangorn were speaking civilly. Probably because they were the two people I was closest to in this world. I would prefer them to get along rather than have them fight. And I hadn't been sure about taking Drake down to meet Fangorn again, with a specific request. But he had behaved well, as had Fangorn.

I had thought good things about this meeting too soon. Just as I began to consider how to wrap things up and end this meeting, Drake looked between Fangorn and me and asked the question. I didn't want to hear it, even though I knew it had to be asked.

"So if you are part dragon, Aine, are you also a shifter?"

Fangorn glanced at me, and I knew he wouldn't say anything. I knew he would leave this to me.

"I haven't tried yet to shift, Drake," I said.

"Why not? Don't you wish to know?"

I resisted the urge to throw something or to slap him. He had no idea. He could not understand.

Then help him. I heard Fangorn's voice in my head.

I don't want him to hate me. The thought came before I could stop it.

He won't.

I wasn't so sure. There didn't seem to be a big hurry to help the dragons. When I'd mentioned this to Fangorn yesterday, he told me that I didn't seem in a hurry to bring anyone down to help them. I got mad then and stomped away. He was right. I was afraid to bring the two sides of me together.

"I do, and at the same time, I do not. Me being a shifter — that is what killed my parents, and all my half siblings for hundreds of years. What if Eilor is not dead? Even if he is dead, what if there someone else who shares the same vision that he had?"

"But I am not Eilor, nor is my father. Or my brother. And we will protect you." Drake didn't hesitate with his response.

"Like you've done since my birth?" I shot back. I knew it was a low blow, but I couldn't help it. I had lived, but how many had died? Right under the noses of these great kings, and no one had noticed.

Drake's brow furrowed in the way that meant he was getting mad. But he didn't say anything.

I continued, slightly ashamed of my outburst of unfair temper. "I want to find out what happened to my mother," I said. That wasn't what I meant to say, but that's what came out. I could see the surprise on the faces of the two men.

Fangorn spoke first. "I don't believe that your mother is alive any longer," he said quietly. I knew he understood.

Everything within me felt tangled into one big knot. Nothing was separate. I looked only at Fangorn. "But she got away, and she got away with my brother. I want to find them. At the very least, I want to find out what happened to them."

Drake spoke again. "Did Eilor ever give you any hint of what happened to them?"

I grudgingly gave him credit for going with the conversation, and not asking more questions than were necessary. That was a good thing about Drake—he got on with the business in front of him. He let the things that could wait, wait. This particular subject could wait forever, as far as I was concerned.

I took a breath. "According to the journals, no. He was furious. He was sure that they had escaped with help from someone in the castle. I believe more than a dozen members of the Court were killed. All because he suspected they might have helped her. Even though," I could feel the heat start to rise in my cheeks, and my hands clenched at my sides. "According to his journals, no one saw them. No one knew they were here. He managed to keep them hidden away up in the far chambers until he took Lionel away. Right before he had Lionel killed." I could not contain my anger.

The thought of my father, the vision that I had gotten reading Eilor's journal, of him touching his baby children, and being taken away, and killed — it inflamed me every time I thought about it.

"You have not tried to shift no, but I think it will happen." This from Fangorn, who'd been watching this interplay quietly.

I whipped my head declared him, "How do you know that?"

"Because your eyes are glowing, and you look very similar to me."

I didn't imagine the satisfaction in his voice.

"If she should begin to shift, will you know?" Drake asked Fangorn.

"I don't know," said Fangorn. "I've never had a child that lived long enough for me to determine whether or not they were shifters. I understand," he said looking at me, "that Lionel, your father was a shifter. Am I correct?" He looked over at Drake, adding, "I only met my son twice. I understand that he shifted in the Human Realm. But I was not part of helping him to shift, and do not know exactly how he came to his ability. It was not with me."

I nodded. Thinking of my father had me seeing his last moments with the picture painted by the journal. My throat closed up with the cry of grief that wanted to escape, and I couldn't speak. When would I be able to think of this and not break down?

"I was not aware that he shifted, although..." Fangorn seemed to be thinking. "I'm not sure that I would've known. Part of being a dragon is part of being a tribe. We are in tune with one another, and the more time we spend together, the more we are tuned. All of us here," he spread out his arms to indicate the other sleeping dragons, "know what is going on. They are not awake. No, and who knows when they may wake again? But when they do it, they will know. They will look at me, or they will see you, and they will know. Because part of being a dragon is sharing the same consciousness."

I never heard this before. "But you talked with Lionel..." I began.

Fangorn was shaking his head before I even finished my thought. "It's not the same. He and I were able to connect, but it was not the proper manner of two dragons. You and I are much closer, daughter."

Drake was obviously still thinking about how dragons shared. "Is that why so many of you were destroyed?" He asked, and I was pleased to hear that his tone was respectful.

After a moment, Fangorn nodded. "While it was never said, I believe so. Because so many of us knew what the others were doing, even if it was from a distance. That is how they were able to determine that those of us here had actively opposed the war. We were deemed…" His lip lifted in a sneer, "safe."

Drake spoke again. "I am sorry," he said. "I believe that you are dealing with me honestly and fairly. As long as you continue to do so, I will do the same. Even if I must say to you things that I know you will not wish to hear. All I ask for in return is the same. Can you honor such a request?"

Fangorn stood quietly, studying Drake. I could feel the intensity of his stare, but I was proud to see that Drake only stared back. He didn't shrink, or back away. He was a strong man, and I was right in believing that he would be a strong king.

"I will do that, son of Jharak," he said.

Drake stepped closer to the cage, sticking out his hand. "Then will you take my hand, and pledge with me? And one other thing," he said, allowing Fangorn to take his hand.

"Yes?" Fangorn asked gripping Drake's hand tightly.

"Please call me Drake," Drake said.

"Very well, Drake," Fangorn said formally.

How he managed to sound formal and at ease at the same time was a skill I wanted to learn.

"Now, may I see the ring?" Fangorn asked.

Drake pulled the ring from a pouch at his belt. He stopped before handing it to Fangorn. "This shocked my father when he touched it, but it hasn't done that to me. I'll be interested to see how it reacts to you."

"You're talking as though the ring has a life of its own," I said.

"It does," Fangorn responded. "I helped to craft this. It is designed to bring the fae who wears it together with the Dragon Realm. While Eilor is the only one who has worn it thus far, it had to be made in such a manner that it could help any fae who wore the crown."

"I haven't been crowned." Drake frowned.

"But you will be." Fangorn held out his hand.

Drake dropped the ring into it. The silence stretched as we waited for Fangorn.

He held it close to his face and sniffed. I felt Drake start next to me at that. I was used to the idea that

Fangorn employed his sense of smell along with his other senses more regularly than the fae did.

Then he looked at it and closed his eyes. The ring began to glow in his hand, but when Fangorn opened his eyes again, the glow winked out.

"It is the correct ring, and oddly, it has a memory. Once you wear it, Drake, you will need to allow it to share. I believe that there will be a great deal that will be revealed in regards to all that Eilor has done."

"It shows everything?" I asked. The thought of all my history being laid bare—

Fangorn must have heard my thoughts. "No, not everything. But things that Eilor used the magic of the Realm for—those are shown. It's not an exact showing, daughter," he said to me. "But it may help to understand what has been done. It may provide answers for helping the Realm."

Fangorn reached out from the bars and brushed at my arm. I wanted to lean into him, but I didn't want to do this in front of Drake. My concerns were not open for discussion.

I gave Fangorn a grateful look, or at least what I hoped was grateful, and then glanced at Drake. He didn't seem to have noticed our interaction, but I'd learned that Drake saw a lot, even if he didn't comment. He was in deep thought.

Finally, he looked up. "You're right, Fangorn. We

don't have the time right now to examine all the things the ring may have been used for. But we will. May I ask for your help with this? Even once you are no longer a regular resident of...My castle?"

I noted that Drake stumbled over the *my* part of the question. I refrained from smiling because I knew he still struggled with the idea that he was about to be a king.

Fangorn nodded. "I will. While you may not believe me, I want to see this Realm in a better place. I have seen firsthand the damage a ruler like Eilor can wreak."

"I believe you," Drake said immediately.

I tuned out as Drake and Fangorn talked more of the specifics of the ring. All I could think was that I might be able to learn about my family the way I wished. How it happened didn't matter to me.

My thoughts were interrupted by Drake.

"We should probably go back, Aine," he said. "Guests will be here before we know it." Then Drake looked at Fangorn and bowed. "I thank you for your help in this matter, Lord Fangorn."

I could feel that Fangorn was pleased.

"I am glad to be a help to my Realm, My lord king," he said, with a bow of his head.

I thought my heart might burst at that moment. I'd been so worried about how Drake and Fangorn would get along. The first meeting had been rather tense. Now, however, they were both going out of their way to be civil and decent to one another. I needed to make sure that this fact made it to Jharak's ears.

"I'll start up, so that you may say your goodbyes," Drake said to me. He gave Fangorn another small nod, and then he headed across the cavern to the stairs.

We both watched as he walked up and then disappeared around the stairway.

"Thank you, daughter, for your efforts to help me," Fangorn said.

I leaned against the bars, letting him put an arm around me. "I'm scared," I said. I knew I wouldn't have to explain why.

"He's not going to condemn you," Fangorn said. "He also comes from a non-traditional background in the eyes of the fae. I would imagine it has not been easy for him, either. He will understand, and more importantly, he will not condemn you."

I pulled away. "I hope you're right."

"I think I am. Now, go, my daughter. Be well." His hand brushed over my head.

I could feel his...affection? Love? In that touch.

Love, his voice said in my head.

I didn't have the words. I looked up, and I knew that he could see the welling in my eyes. My throat closed with an ache. I squeezed his hand and turned to head up the stairs, taking them two at a time. Not easy in my dress, but I managed to catch up with Drake.

As Drake and I slowly walked up the stairwell together, neither of us spoke. I figured he was as lost in his thoughts as I was in mine. I felt like the meeting had gone well, even though we didn't resolve anything regarding Eilor. It was obvious that Drake wasn't sure what to believe in regards to Eilor being alive or dead.

It was equally obvious to both Fangorn myself that he might be alive, dead body proof notwithstanding. Fangorn was still in the cage. The bars still didn't open. There was no easy solution to this, so I resigned it to one of those things that would have to be answered with time. At least now, Drake would be on his guard. That was the important thing.

Drake finally spoke, "Thank you for bringing me down to see him without blindfolds," he said. "I appreciate the trust that you placed in me."

"You can't tell your father or your brother that you know how to reach them. Or I will ban you from the door," I said.

"But when we bring Taranath to them, he will know," Drake said

"Then we can blindfold him," I said. "I will not risk them, not for anything."

"I understand," he said. "But I have another matter which I need to speak to you about."

We finally reached the top of the stairs.

"Would you prefer to come to my rooms?" I asked, feeling rather shy. I let no one into my rooms, much less Drake.

He nodded. "I need to speak openly with you, and..." he looked around as I led us out of the locked corridor, "We both know that castles have ears."

"That they do," I said.

Neither of us spoke as I led the way back to my room. Once I opened the door, and he stepped in and closed it behind him, I walked towards my sitting area.

Off of my sleeping area, I had a very lovely sitting area that opened up to the lawns that went away from the castle. They were overgrown and had been left untended for years. Eilor had not had much time for keeping the gardens tidy. It seemed the more I learned, the more I realized that the resources of the Dragon Realm went towards whatever was that Eilor thought he was doing.

"Why don't we sit in here?" I asked. Somehow, the thought of Drake in my bedroom area may be uncomfortable. He walked in and took a seat.

"What is it you wish to speak about?" I asked. I sat across from him so that I could watch him.

"I spoke with my father today," Drake said. "One of the things that he mentioned, and I think he's correct, is that we must get things back to some normalcy here in the Dragon Realm. Would you not agree?"

It was amazing to me that we were thinking along the same lines. Before going to see Fangorn, I'd been thinking about how the Realm needed so much and had not been taken care of.

"I would," I said. I wasn't going to tell him we were sharing ideas. I was also very glad that we weren't revisiting anything more personal.

"To do that, I need your help," Drake said frankly. "I don't know enough about the daily running of a castle to be effective at it. Sadly," he grinned unexpectedly at me, "What I am learning is that I was very well taken care of in the Goblin Castle. To even come close to that sort of comfort, I'm going to need your help, to not only choose people to help me do this but find ways to make the daily life of the inhabitants of this Realm better."

"I think that would go a long way," I said slowly. "The day-to-day concerns of the people who live here was not anything that Eilor thought about, not from what I could see."

Drake got up, obviously not able to sit still. He walked in front of the windows, hands behind his back, staring out of them, but not seeing them gardens below. Or so it seemed.

"Jharak suggested that we talk to the merchants,

the people who run the marketplace. Again, something I hadn't even considered. When is the market held here? I haven't been able to determine that."

I sat back, thinking. I have never been to a market. I didn't even know if we had one. "I don't know," I said.

Drake nodded, as though I had confirmed something he'd been suspecting. "Very well, then we will need to speak to the basic needs of the people here. You recall my lists?"

That made me laugh. "I realize that you showed me a great honor in allowing me to actually look over your lists, but as you carry them around like your nearest and dearest, they are rather hard to forget. If the rest of the Court gets wind of them, they're going to freeze whenever they see you writing something," I said.

At that, he did turn and glare at me. "I can't keep them all straight! I'm used to seeing goblins, not a bunch of simpering fae. The fae in my father's kingdom do not act this way." He crossed his arms with a huff.

I had to laugh again. He looked so aggrieved. "You just don't know how well you had it, goblin boy," I said teasingly.

Drake laughed a little at that, his posture relaxing. "No, I didn't. Who would've thought that the Goblin Realm would've been the pinnacle of sophistication?"

"Are the goblins not sophisticated?" I asked. I'd never seen a goblin. I never saw anyone other than the fae and dragons. When we'd visited the Goblin Realm, it had been brief, and there had been no interaction with anyone in the Castle. Jharak wanted Drake to get to the Dragon Realm quickly, without people realizing what he might be up to.

Drake burst out laughing at my words. "You've never met goblins, have you?"

As I shook my head, he laughed again.

"Then we shall have to remedy that. I'll take you to the Goblin Castle for longer than just a quick stop, and you'll see why I'm so frustrated. No, they are definitely not sophisticated. What they are is very pleasant, and helpful, and enjoyable creatures to be around. Most fae don't think much of them, but Brennan loves them. After I lived with him for a time, I learned to love them too. They're very open, and there is no guile or malice in them." His face shuttered for a moment. I wondered what he was thinking.

Then Drake spoke again. "Well, for the most part, that's how they are. There are occasionally those who choose a different path." The same shuttered look remained on his face.

"Do the goblins have a marketplace?" I wondered what caused the change in expression.

"Do they have a marketplace? By the sun and

moon, yes, they have a marketplace. They are great lovers of earrings and trinkets and baubles, and they love to go during their time off and haggle and shop. I miss the goblin that was in charge of my rooms," he said wistfully.

"Will you bring him here?" I asked.

He shook his head. "No, she wouldn't be happy. She has a large extended family, and she's very close to them. No," he sighed, "I shall have to make do with this poor fae boy that is waiting on me now. I can't tell if he's scared of me or waiting for me to do something incredibly stupid."

I laughed. "You know, if you don't like your body servant, you don't have to keep him."

He threw up his hands. "Yes, but if I get rid of him, then what will happen to him? He'll be given hell down in the staff quarters, and considered something less than, damaged or failed goods."

For someone not in the Dragon Realm for very long, Drake it picked up the way that the staff was treated here.

Drake continued, "But you will help me? Will you help me find the appropriate fae within the castle? Figure out where the court, or whatever it is they're hiding, *is*, and start to set to rights the daily life here? I know things here will be upended for the next week or so, but Jharak feels this is a good step."

"Your father told you all that?" It gave me a different view of Jharak. The Jharak that I had seen was stoic and extraordinarily sad. He'd just seen his son die, and his wife turn from him. He had nothing to celebrate, no reason to even extend the barest of civility to me. But he'd done that, and been extremely gracious. I realized now, however, I had not seen him at his best.

"Yes. He said that one of the easiest ways to begin healing a Realm was to help the Realm get back to some semblance of normal. Unfortunately, I'm not sure what passes for normal around here. Given the fact that you can't ever remember having a market day, we may have to start on a much smaller scale."

I got up from where I sat and joined him where he stood looking out the window. I looked at the neglected gardens, and the outside of the castle grounds, all of which looked as though they hadn't been cared for in many years. "I don't think so, Drake. I think making a big statement is precisely what you need. The people of this Realm are used to a king who cares not for their concerns. Who is not interested in the things that are worrisome or joyful to them. Why do you think that Carlianah was so eager to get out of here? It wasn't just because she loved the son of that fae courtier. It was because she wanted to live somewhere where you didn't have to worry about what the mood of the king was."

"So what do you suggest then?"

"Why don't we start with the castle grounds?" I nodded towards the neglect we could see right in front of us. One thing I'd seen at the Goblin Castle was the grounds. They were well-kept, and even from a distance, looked inviting. I'd been looking out my window lately, wanting to see the same sort of thing.

We smiled at one another in perfect understanding.

14

DRAKE

*H*e stretched and then got up. He felt that he'd been living in this study. Thank the stars the chair was comfortable.

He realized he hadn't seen Aine since they'd been down to see Fangorn. She had taken the bit between her teeth, to use a phrase he described his stallion with. They had talked for a while in her chambers, and from what he could see, she'd been working ever since. It had only been a short time, but he found that he missed her.

Anyway, her mad efforts would need to stop soon. His father was coming tonight.

Probably not a good idea to mention to Aine that she reminded him of his horse. She'd take his head off.

He thought back to their conversation in her

rooms. She had gone from her chamber and immediately went to the kitchens. He'd followed her.

She sought out the head chef and the keeper of the keys, a man and a woman who were married, and together, ran the castle. Drake hadn't realized the head chef was a man. All he'd seen were women.

The three heads had bent together, and he realized at that point that he was not needed. So he'd left—fled, actually—and been in his study ever since.

It was time to find her, and see what she'd been up to. He found that he missed seeing her. Well, of course, he missed seeing her. Aine was his favorite person within the Realm. Even without the fact that he'd kissed her.

When had that happened? Yes, he found her attractive, but when had she become his favorite person?

He didn't want to think about it. Not right now. Later, maybe.

He ventured out of his study, stretching again with pure pleasure at the mere fact of being out of his chair. He had only assumed that Aine had taken charge, but standing in the corridor, looking out over his — well, his soon-to-be castle, he could see that his assumption was indeed correct.

For the first time since he arrived at the Dragon Castle, there was a sense of bustle, of connectedness, of contentment. This reminded him in many ways of the way that the Goblin Castle felt. It also made him realize that was one of the reasons he hadn't wanted to be here, initially. It lacked the things that made it a home.

He knew had been correct in trusting Aine to make this a home. In spite of her declarations that she didn't understand what was normal and what wasn't, she seemed to have an excellent grasp of what was needed.

Going on the idea that his assumptions were leading him in the right direction, he headed down the corridor towards the stairs that would lead to the kitchen. As he made his way down the stairwell, he passed two different fae who looked to be staff, rather than members of the court. Both of them gave him a shy smile, and the woman actually dropped a little curtsy.

That was new. Although the coronation was a mere two days away, so it made sense.

Was this how Brennan felt? While he had never desired to be a king, he'd often wondered how it would feel. The last month or so, he decided that he didn't like it. Until he felt he had no choice but to do as Jharak asked. But this difference, this change, this might not be so bad. The people he'd seen thus far were happy.

And that was worth the effort. Even if there were bad times and challenges ahead.

He passed several more staff members, noting that they all had an improved sense of happiness. They moved with a sense of purpose, and not one of them looked afraid that he might burst into some sort of rage or fit. No one looked afraid. That was a huge improvement from when he'd arrived.

It had to be Aine.

The next question would be, how would the courtiers behave? Or rather, his courtiers? He should probably start to think of them that way. He hadn't seen much of them. Once the coronation was announced, many had gone to their family homes. Now that he'd spoken with Jharak, he realized that it was no doubt to prepare. Get a dress. That sort of thing.

The staff was different. This felt like the staff at home. His former home. He realized with a pang how much he was going to miss the Goblin Castle. He wondered if he would offend to their dying day, any of the staff here if he brought some of his goblin staff. Not the woman who'd been in charge of his rooms. She wouldn't want to leave. But some of her assistants—some of them had been with him since he and Brennan first came to the Goblin Castle. Then he remembered what he'd told Aine. He sighed. They wouldn't be happy here. They preferred to be close to their clans and their families.

No, he would need to make a new family of his own. He sighed again, more heavily this time. He knew what that meant. After maybe a hundred years or so, Nerida would start nagging him as she'd been nagging Brennan for the last three or four hundred years. It would take her that long to forgive him. Or perhaps not. Jharak seemed cautiously optimistic. But only cautiously.

As he entered the kitchens, and the various cooks and kitchen staff saw him, there were nods and bows. He stopped, realizing he didn't know where the hell he was going.

"Where would I find the Lady Aine?"

The young man closest to him pointed towards the other end of the kitchen. "She's in there with the head cook, sire," he said, adding that last word almost shyly. Drake noted how young he sounded. How young he looked. He wondered if he was getting old. Then he told himself to quit being stupid, and get on with it.

He nodded his thanks to the young man along with a smile and headed in the direction the man pointed. At the end of the kitchen, he saw an open door and within he could hear Aine, along with several other voices.

He almost walked in, but he stopped at the

doorway and observed. He must have made some noise because four heads turned around to look and see who was there. Three of them immediately ducked into a curtsy. All except Aine. She smiled, and he realized he hadn't seen her smile in some time. He was pleased—very pleased—to see it.

There were a lot of realizations for him today. He wasn't sure that he could manage much more. At least not without a grueling session in the practice yard.

"My lord Drake, I am so glad that you're here." Aine stepped over and took his arm, drawing him into the conversation.

She gestured at parchment on the rough table in front of them. He took a quick glance around the room. This must be the housekeeper's room, there were bits of paper stuck to the wall, and various boxes and bottles and jars stacked up along the walls. He brought his attention back to the table, to see what it was that Aine was pointing at.

"As you requested, My lord," Aine said respectfully, "I have entered into talks with the household staff as to what would be necessary to start holding a market. As I previously informed you, there has not been a market here for as long as anyone can remember."

All the things in the room were forgotten as he contemplated what she just said. "You mean to tell me that there has never been a market here? How is commerce handled? How does food make its way throughout the Realm? How does anything make its way throughout the Realm?" He looked around, not only at Aine but at the other three in the room with her.

He recognized the taller, heavyset man as the chef. The woman was the keeper of the keys, and he wasn't sure who the third person, another woman, was. All looked slightly older than he. Which meant nothing.

"How long have the three of you been here?" He asked. He hoped he didn't sound as accusatory as he thought he did. That would do nothing to get the answers out of them he needed.

All three glanced at one another, almost as afraid they might use the wrong answer.

Then the woman, the keeper of the keys, spoke up. "I've been here for over eight hundred years, My lord. They've been here almost as long." She indicated the man and the woman on either side of her.

Only slightly older than he was. "Why has there been no market, why has there been no attempts at standardizing any trade, or barter? Or anything?"

More glances among the three. This time it was the woman to the left of the keeper who spoke. "The King, the old King," she amended with a sheepish look at Drake, "he felt they were... What was his word, Polly?

Inappropriate?" She looked over the keeper of the keys.

Polly. That was the keeper of the keys. He realized he didn't even know their names. It was very lowering to be faced with multiple realizations of where he was not doing his best every single day. He thought himself a smart man, an educated man. But in the course of half an hour, he'd learned how just uneducated he was.

Polly nodded. "Yes, he didn't feel it was appropriate. He felt it was demeaning, somehow, for us to engage in any trade."

"Well, that's just stupid," Drake said before he could even stop himself. "I've lived in both the Fae Castle and the Goblin Castle my entire life, and both of the kings and the fae queen shopped in the marketplace. With all due respect," he gave a nod towards the three fae, "I think your King was incorrect."

The chef nodded vigorously. "My lord, I am so glad to hear you say that. It is very difficult for me to get the fresh food that is needed to feed everyone in the castle. And with such large numbers, it is a full-time job procuring everything that we need."

Drake tapped his finger against his leg, thinking. "Would it not be a full-time job anyway?" He asked

The chef nodded. "Indeed, My lord. But would be

much less of a full-time job if we had a market that was readily available, where we might place orders, look at the produce, get to know suppliers."

He glanced over at Aine and saw that she had a slight smile on her face. Unlike some of the smiles he'd seen from her in the past, while rare, this one reached her eyes. He found that it warmed him with from within, and made his neck feel warm. He resisted the urge to scratch at it and continued speaking with the chef.

Within ten minutes, he and Aine had arranged with the trio to begin advertising for people to be in the marketplace. He'd made sure the chef, the key keeper, and the third woman, who was the assistant head chef, were prepared for the coronation. It was a relief to hear they had it in hand, having planned for some time.

He wished he'd paid more attention when Brennan dealt with the castle steward. The steward was the person who handled the taxes, and any fees, and all the other treasury sort of items that Drake paid no attention to. He wondered again if he could get Brennan to lend him his steward. Then he thought better of asking for such a favor. Brennan already wanted his mage back.

"Is there anyone else other than the man I dismissed that could serve as a steward?" Drake asked

Aine as they left the kitchens. He figured she'd know better than anyone else.

She frowned, thinking. "I don't know. There has to be someone, but I have a suspicion, Drake, that as we dive into this, we're going to upset some apple carts."

This was something that Drake understood. "You mean Eilor's negligence allowed for someone else to enrich themselves?" He asked slowly.

She nodded. "I do. I think it's time that you held a court session. In preparation for the coronation," she said.

"What in the name of all the demons is a court?" Asked Drake. He didn't like the sound of it. It sounded like it involves formal clothing and a great deal of formality. And very little directness, or openness, or honesty.

"Most of the court is here, Drake," she said.

"They are? I thought they'd all left, gone to their own homes."

"They did, but they've been arriving all day. The ceremony *is* happening fairly imminently," She said.

She had a very earnest look on her face, and he found that he enjoyed it. He was finding that he was thinking about her at inappropriate times and in inappropriate ways. He wasn't sure he like that either. That kiss, the way she'd felt in his arms—he needed to stop this.

"Oh, so now you're the expert on the court?"

She reached up and slapped him in the back of the head. "I'm an expert on a lot more things that you realize, Drake. I was both here, and invisible," she said, glaring at him. "That allowed me to see a lot more than most people, who drew attention wherever they went."

Drake considered her words. They made sense. "All right. I'll bow to your superior intelligence, in this one instance," he warned. "What does this mean I have to do?" He ignored the fact that he enjoyed her touching him willingly, even it was merely a slap on the head. Although perhaps he would need to caution her to not do that in front of other people.

"Well, you're not the king, yet. But you are... The regent? Yes, that would be a good name for you. The Regent. We'll send out an invitation today, to all of the members of the court, all the lords and ladies who are present, from," she bowed elaborately towards him. "My lord, Drake, Regent of the Fae King. A meeting before the pomp and circumstance of the coronation."

He grimaced, although he had to admit it had a ring to it. "I suppose that's not too horrible," he said. "Can you arrange the invitations? Since I still have no steward," he sighed.

She turned towards him, the curiosity evident on her face. "Why do you fear the throne so much, Drake?"

Perhaps it was the simplicity with which she asked, or just that he was feeling like talking to someone, anyone, but he answered her. Or maybe because it was Aine, and she'd allowed him to see so much of her in the last few days. She was...safe. Either way, he didn't hesitate when he spoke. "I never wanted to be a king. I never saw myself as a king. My father, my brother — those are kings. They are formal and correct, and —"

"They are truly fae?" She asked softly.

He stopped right there, in the middle of the corridor. He looked at her, opened his mouth to retort, but nothing came out.

"Yes," he said simply. Unable to look her in the eyes, not wanting to see the pity or whatever other emotion she had for such a pathetic admittance, he turned and headed back towards the study.

Much safer to stay in there.

15

AINE

I watched Drake stalk off after my simple question. Except it wasn't that simple. I've been listening to him before taking him to meet Fangorn, and an idea had been forming. After he had asked me to help him bring some sense of normalcy back to the Dragon Realm, I hadn't seen him until he came to the kitchen. I've been so involved with discussions with the various members of the castle staff; I had lost track of the fact that he and I hadn't seen one another recently.

Watching him talk with the kitchen staff today, I had seen a different side of Drake. He was interested in what they had to say and engaging. Friendly. Relaxed. Not formal at all. He was very different from his father, or his brother.

He'd been human when he was wished to the Fae Realm. I knew how people looked at me here, in the court. While I'd grown up here with a position that wasn't easily defined, as far as anyone else knew, I was fae like all the rest of them. Even though there was something different about me. In spite of all the rumors surrounding Eilor, I didn't think that people had any idea I was part dragon. The dragon bit would have pushed people over the edge.

With Drake, I thought, watching his shoulders hunch as he got further away from me down the corridor, they knew exactly why he was different. He was human. Well, he had been human. He was human once, but no more. Why did this stick with him for so long?

However, because of that start as a human, he was not expected to take on any of the roles that a man in his position would normally do. All due to starting life as a human.

Sometimes the narrow-mindedness of my fellow fae made me want to kick all of them. Specifically in a place where a kick would be the most instructive. Or at least the most memorable.

As Drake turned the corner, presumably headed to that little hole in the wall study of his, I sighed. I knew exactly how it felt. I knew exactly what it meant not to feel like you belong. Except, unlike me, Drake had made a place for himself. Where, in spite of his not belonging, he belonged. And now he was here, in another place where he felt he didn't belong. Where he would have to make a place for himself. I hoped the rest of the court would give him a chance. The staff were pleased with his concern for them, and I'd seen an immediate change in them.

I stood, staring at him. Or rather, where he'd gone. For a man who prized openness, honesty, and blunt talk, there was a great deal he kept shuttered and hidden.

That was not mine to sort out. I decided that I would go down into the kitchens once more, find the keeper of the keys. She would know who it made it their business to profit off of how the last King had run things. She'd have a good idea of who would be a decent, honest steward. She'd also probably know best how to get the word out about holding a gathering this evening just for the members of the Dragon Court.

I was going to help Drake get rid of those that wouldn't help this Realm come to life again.

At the thought of helping out Drake, my thoughts went to a place where I had not expected them to. A place I wasn't sure I wanted my thoughts to visit. In spite of that, I traced the lines of his shoulders, down to his thin and trim waist, then his strong and muscular legs in my mind's eye. No. I shook my head. *Stop it.*

What was I doing? Why was I thinking of him this way? Who was I, to have such thoughts? My eyes traced where he had been before he disappeared around the corner, and I felt the corners of my mouth tilt up.

No matter how one looked at Drake, and I've been looking at him from a number of angles recently—he always looked good.

I shook my head again. I needed to go down and see Fangorn, put my mind back where it belongs. To tell him of what we were doing. To focus on getting this Realm better. And to free him.

And maybe myself.

I realized I hadn't been down there at all today. Fangorn would be worried. The kitchens could wait. It wouldn't take that long to talk to Polly. Fangorn was used to seeing me daily. I hurried to the corridor and opened up the false wall, and then down the stairs. I moved so fast that the lanterns couldn't keep up with me.

As I entered the cavern, I called out, "Fangorn! Are you awake?"

A moment of silence, and then, "I am," his voice came from the back of his cage. I heard a great shuffling, a much more massive noise than if it was Fangorn in his fae form. As I approached his cage, and the lanterns nearby lit themselves, I could see that

Fangorn had shifted back into his dragon form. His eyes were larger than normal and glowing green as he turned to face me.

"Daughter," his voice rumbled through my bones, "are you well? I was surprised not to see you this morning. Is aught amiss?"

"No, Grandfather," I replied. He'd told me I could call him *Father* if I wished, and I thought he would enjoy it. I wasn't yet comfortable with that idea. He seemed to understand, as he did not press me.

He also told me that it was a dragon way to refer to all the children of your line as either daughter or son. While I wasn't following his traditions, I didn't think I was offending him, even though I didn't want to hurt his feelings.

His great blue head lifted as he tilted it to study me better. "There is something different about you, Aine. What has changed?"

I had not seen Fangorn in dragon form very often. When I did, I noted that unlike when he was in fae form, he tended to be more direct, a little sparser with his words. Not that he was overly wordy to begin with. But when you dealt with the dragons in their true form, there was a lot less room for diplomacy, lying, or any subterfuge. Their words were chosen carefully, and with skill. Hence the reputation for manipulation. With smaller amounts of words, one became very careful and crafty with the words chosen.

Knowing what I had been thinking about, knowing where my thoughts had gone to, I felt my face blush. I looked down, and said, "Nothing has happened. Why do you ask?"

"Come closer," he said. His snout came close to the edge of the cage, right up next to the bars.

I knew he would not hurt me. I had no fear of being eaten, I thought, stifling a giggle. Drake had mentioned such a concern at some point. Gently, as though a soft spring breeze wafted through the cavern, he sniffed me. I felt the gentle *whiffle*, and stood still, allowing his scrutiny.

"You are not entirely open with me, my daughter," he said. "You've reached a new phase in your maturity. Who is it that you wish to mate with?"

I jumped back, my mouth open, my eyes wide. "Fangorn! What kind of question is that?"

"An honest one, Aine. It is my job, as the last of your family, to make sure that you are situated properly. There is no shame in mating. As I've told you, I had several mates. All of them were wonderful and extraordinary in their own ways. I do not think," he mused, a puff of smoke drifting up from his nostrils, "that the fae have the same ideas about mating as dragons. Or is my information incorrect?"

"I don't know! I've never thought about that myself!"

"Oh, but you think of it now. If you are thinking of it, the dragon part of you will soon take over."

Did I hear satisfaction in his tone? I put my hands on my hips and took a step closer to the bars so I could properly glare. "And you're happy about that?"

I never imagined what it would look like to see a dragon shrug, but Fangorn managed it. I saw his massive shoulders go up and down, looking for all the world like a man casually shrugging. Maybe it was a male thing. They just all instinctively knew how to do it.

"The sooner your dragon side integrates with your fae and human side, the sooner we will know whether or not you can shift. That is a question that I think you would want to be answered, before letting anyone else know about us." His dragon face looked like it was smiling.

"It will also allow for you to move on into your maturity."

I took a deep breath, the flush fading for my face. I tried to step away from how embarrassing this was, having this sort of discussion with your grandfather. It was times like these I felt such a difference from him. Dragons were...different. And apparently, they talked about mating as though it were like having seconds on dinner.

"Yes, that is something I would like to know." My face felt like it would burst into flames at any moment. Maybe if I focused on the shifting part of things, he'd stop talking about mating. Because that sent my thoughts directly to...I stopped myself.

His eyes swiveled back down towards me, and I felt skewered. They were gleaming very brightly. They glowed in the relative darkness of the cavern, torches notwithstanding. He almost looked as though he was laughing.

"Which part would you like to know, daughter? The part about shifting, or the part about mating?"

The heat returned to my face with ferocity, and I looked down at the floor. "Shifting." Then I looked up because he was making a noise that was what a dragon would sound like if it were laughing.

"Stop it! This is difficult!" I nearly shouted.

He laughed harder. I glared.

He looked at me and stopped his laughing. "Your eyes are so bright they look as though they might burst into flames. It is good to see the eyes of another dragon looking at me, daughter. It's been a long time."

I felt some of my anger slip away. Was he—? I shook my finger at him. "Don't change the subject, and try and get me to feel sorry for you after you just embarrassed me! You may sense something different about me, but I do *not* want to discuss mating or men or anything like that with you right now. I would like to discuss shifting, but...But that's it."

He studied me for a moment. That moment stretched out, and I wondered if I'd gone too far regarding dragon etiquette. "It is not my intention to make you uncomfortable, Aine. So we shall stick to shifting." He closed his eyes.

It was so odd seeing a dragon employing all the things—like facial expressions--I thought of as belonging to fae.

"Does the integration get easier over time?" I asked before I could help myself.

The eyes opened lazily. "Yes. It does. I can shift back and forth with only a thought. Once you reach that level, you must take care not to shift merely because your thoughts are focused on how you would handle something in your other form."

"Oh. That could get..." I began.

"Yes. It can. It does. It will before you learn to manage it."

"That's if I can even shift," I grumbled. I hadn't been sure in the past how I felt about having such an ability. Particularly as I'd known the moment I shifted, Eilor would have more and more he wanted from me.

Now, however, if I shifted, it would be for my purposes alone.

But wouldn't that open me up to the desires and schemes of others?

Yes, Fangorn said.

"Stop that!" I spoke out loud. "That's distracting. And I'm not sure I care for it."

He regarded me neutrally and then spoke. "That is one of the ways we communicate. What is it that bothers you?"

"Having someone in my head at all times," I said immediately. "I have grown up essentially being studied. I have never really had the privacy of my person. The only place left to me was my thoughts."

It surprised me how strongly I felt. But with each passing day that took me further from the life I'd lived up until now, I became more aware of how poorly Eilor had treated me. How wrong he'd been in how he forced me to live. How much of myself hadn't been my own.

I was protective of this new self, fiercely so. That surprised me, too. I'd not been allowed to feel strongly about anything. Even strong emotion was something new, something to be cherished.

Fangorn listened to my thoughts. In spite of the declaration I'd just made, I didn't mind. These thoughts were so new, so foreign to me, that it was challenging to articulate them. Having someone who could—

I looked at him. *All right*, I said mentally. *I get your point. It is—it can be an advantage. But how do you allow for the right of another to have their own thoughts?*

We learn to turn away, to allow the dragons near us to have that privacy. It's just easier to speak without words at times. Wouldn't you agree?

I looked at him. *How come I can't look into your head like you seem to look into mine?*

He shrugged. *Because the idea of being in someone else's thoughts is nothing that has ever occurred to you.*

I thought about this. "Can you read the thoughts of the fae?"

"No," he rumbled. "I get a sense, but it's not like it is with other dragons."

"Good," I sagged in relief a bit. "I don't know if I can handle being privy to the thoughts of those around me. It's hard enough to be around people as it is. Toss their thoughts in, and I may never come out of my room again."

Fangorn laughed. "It does take time. As much as I want to be free, I have been thinking about how it would be. To be free," He looked over my head, seeing something other than the cavern we were in. "It's a different world than when I was put in here. My kind —for the most part—are no more. I worry that should I go free, I will put myself in a different sort of cage."

"Do you think they," I indicated the rest of the dragons with a nod, "Would want to be free?"

"Does any being wish to spend a life in a cage?" He responded immediately. "Although I do not know. Their thoughts have been hazy to me for many years. They very well might wish to live out their days here, slumbering." Again with the massive shrug. "None of this is a consideration until we know if the doors will ever open."

"I know," I said. I felt guilty that I couldn't—

"Do not take responsibility for actions that were not yours," Fangorn cut off my thoughts. "May we speak of another concern?"

"Of course," I said. I was relieved that we were off the subject of all aspects of my personal life.

Fangorn smiled a toothy, wide dragon smile. He'd probably heard me. But he didn't tease me further. "I am ready to meet the mage you and the new king mentioned. Will you bring him today?"

I considered for a moment. I had promised to help Drake, and his family was arriving tonight. But—

"Yes. I will go and find him now."

"Thank you, Aine. I know that you feel pulled in many directions. I am grateful you see me as one of the directions worth your attention." He inclined his head.

Fangorn was not usually so gracious. He was always polite, but he had a tone of command that was enviable. This sounded appreciative.

"I am," he rumbled. "I had forgotten what it was like to have someone who cared what happened to one. And I believe that I might have been overbearing initially. I do not wish you to feel you must do anything. I also want you to know I am glad you are part of my life. Even if my life never goes beyond here, I am grateful for you, Aine," he finished.

The tears filled my eyes. "I am so very grateful for you, too," I said. "I have never had a family before."

He held out a claw to me. I stepped into it, letting him curl it around me. He rested the part of his snout that fit through the bars on mine. No words were needed. The sense of belonging, of being a part of something was indescribable.

He let go of me. "Now go. I know that your tasks are great today."

I hurried up the long stairway. Once I'd locked the corridor behind me, I went in search of Taranath.

16

DRAKE

*H*e couldn't settle himself. His brief conversation with Aine had left him feeling on edge. He had not been this jumpy since he was young, before Brennan became the Goblin King. It was ridiculous.

Aine was right, of course. He needed to hold court, this evening. The rest of the family was descending— like an outburst of some plague, he thought. But it would make a much bigger impression—or spectacle —if he could call the courtiers to task with two of the other kings of the Realm with him.

While Drake didn't long for a crown, even now, he appreciated the strategy of having the fae wearing them in one's corner. Aine had been right about not feeling fae enough as well. He didn't want to admit it, but there it was.

Drake had heard the whispers all his life. They were not as loud as they'd once been, but the whispers —and whisperers—were still there. He anticipated hearing outright snide commentary at some point. Perhaps Jharak already had. Which made this idea of holding a court session even more appropriate. He'd get a chance to see who might turn against him if the occasion to rebel arose.

As he went to his rooms, he called for the young man—Trevan—who waited on him and requested a scribe. He wondered what the scribes did all day because one was there almost immediately.

"Please invite all the courtiers who are here, as well as any who might be within the town walls, to a session of Court this evening," Drake told Harald, the scribe. "I realize this is last minute, so please let them know that it is not necessary to observe court formality."

Harald's eyes widened. "All the courtiers, My lord? Tonight?"

Drake nodded. "Yes. It is no mark against them if they are unable to attend. I have only just decided to hold Court today. I understand that my decision may not work with the plans of some. But I want to offer this to the Realm before the coronation." He smiled so that Harald would know he meant what he said.

Or at least, he hoped Harald knew it. It didn't matter, he thought. His motives may be questioned now, but they wouldn't be forever. He would start off as he wished to rule. Let the court think what it would.

Drake had no idea if the Dragon Court followed similar rules to those of the Fae Court. He knew when Jharak held Court it was pretty formal. He didn't want that. He wondered if it was more his mother or his father who preferred the formality, or if they were just following tradition.

As the scribe hurried away, an expression of panic barely concealed, Drake let his thoughts go back to his conversation with Aine. Much of what he'd grappled with since he got here was based on the childhood concerns that came with occasional reminders as an adult that he was not quite good enough.

He hadn't thought of it for years until Ailla had brought it to the forefront. That he was an outcast, a person to be mocked and jeered at.

Ailla. Drake sighed. Why did that hateful woman still bring a pang to his chest? Surely he didn't still care for her? Not when thoughts of Aine came to him as they had been. Suddenly, and with a fondness that he ought to find alarming.

But he didn't. So why the wistful thoughts about the crazy woman who had made him behave in ways that left only shame? Did he still care for her?

No. As he'd been thinking on this for a while, Drake realized that he cared that he'd finally allowed himself to trust someone other than Brennan and it had been a ruse. He'd also been untrue to his brother. That aspect of the matter stuck in hard, like a knife to the heart. There was no getting away from it. Not only that, she'd used that closeness to hurt him—to try and rip a part of him away.

While he'd spoken with both Brennan and Iris—which had been rather awkward—and he knew that neither held any resentment towards him, it didn't ease his guilt. Worse, he didn't know what it would take for him to ease it, either.

Drake found the whole thing maddening. He knew that Ailla had been cunning, and had done the things she'd done because she had a plot in mind. He knew that he had been taken in. That was the crux of it.

He should have known better. To be gulled...his pride stung.

He remembered thinking something wasn't right and ignoring those thoughts. Drake hadn't told anyone about that. He did know better, and he'd ignored his doubts.

How did you forgive yourself for knowingly betraying the person in the world you loved more than anyone else? He couldn't tell anyone, had no one to unburden himself to. But he knew his actions.

Drake felt certain that all the lingering chaos he still carried was his to deal with. The cost of his betrayal.

What he hadn't expected was to find that it called into question everything he'd ever thought of himself. It dredged up the old taunts and whispers of his origin. Of not being 'not quite good enough.'

There was no one he could say this to. Not even Iris, with whom he felt comfortable. Even as he knew she wouldn't judge him, he judged himself.

No. This was the cost of his actions. All actions had consequences, and everyone had to deal with them.

This was his lot. He had chosen it, and now he must bear it.

He turned his thoughts from his concerns and called for help again.

Drake sighed. Now he had to figure out what to wear. The Court would be demanding enough. He also needed to face his family.

———

*F*inally, his manservant, Trevan, declared him ready. Drake gazed at himself in the mirror. He was still Drake, but there was something more, something different.

"You look a proper king, if I do say so, My lord,"

Trevan said with great satisfaction. "Best looking king we've had in an age."

He smiled at the young man. "Thank you. I'll try to live up to your standards."

Trevan looked worried until he saw Drake's grin. "I mean no disrespect, My lord. I'll be calling you sire after tomorrow, though."

"No need, Trevan. You're going to have the pleasure of seeing me in all states, so you may keep to 'My lord.'" Drake saw that Trevan looked surprised, so he added, "When it's just the two of us in my chambers."

He didn't imagine the look of relief on the man's face. While he didn't want to be as formal as the Fae Court, he would need to, he supposed, add some formality. Drake sighed. This would become normal after a time.

"Would you like something to eat before everyone arrives?" Trevan asked.

"Good thought. Can you also send the mage Taranath to me?"

Trevan nodded, and Drake went into the small room off his sleeping chamber that he was using for... well, he didn't know. But after Aine had cleaned out the rooms, and had a veritable herd of mages go through making sure nothing of Eilor remained, she'd directed the furnishing of the room. This had two comfortable chairs and a chaise lounge. He wasn't sure what he'd do with a chaise, but it didn't seem worth it to argue with Aine. It would do to sit in peace and eat.

He stared out the window of the small room. It had a nice view of the gardens. Aine had been correct in that the entire Dragon Castle was potentially attractive, but he could see the neglect on the place. Good thing he'd already added the grounds on the list of tasks to address. He needed to speak with Taranath to see what magic could be used to help things along.

The door to his chambers burst open, and he whirled around, feeling for his sword. Then he remembered he wasn't wearing it.

Trevan looked as though he'd been running. "My lord, the Fae King has arrived."

Drake stood up straighter and squared his shoulders. "It's the lot of them, isn't it?"

Trevan nodded, glancing over his shoulder. Before he could say anything else, a voice rang out.

"Where is my son?"

Nerida had arrived. That was the last thing he expected.

"You may bring a light meal for all," Drake told Trevan, who nodded, and then all but sidled from the room, making jerky motions of his head as he passed Nerida, Jharak, Brennan, and Iris.

Iris watched him as he shut the door. Then she

looked at Drake. "What have you done to that poor guy? He looked terrified!"

Drake laughed, walking to embrace his father. "It wasn't me who was doing the terrifying."

"Will you not greet me?" Nerida's voice was cool.

Drake stepped away from Jharak and regarded his mother with what he hoped was a congenial expression. It wasn't necessary to start off with a fight.

"I am your son again?" He asked.

Nerida's nostrils flared, but she didn't snap at him. "You have always been my son."

Drake let his gaze wander a little to see Iris behind his mother. If they were in the same room and Iris hadn't gone after Nerida, some peace must have been met. *It would have been nice to be included,* he thought.

"Somehow, Mother, I wasn't so sure." He hated that his voice came out hard. And that no one else was speaking. Damn them.

Nerida held his gaze, and then her head dropped. "I am sorry," she said. She kept her head down, and then looked back up at him. "I was wrong, and I am sorry. I behaved badly towards you. I have no excuse. I..." She looked away.

Watching her expressions play across her face, Drake could tell that this wasn't easy for Nerida. For all the grief her words and actions caused, he couldn't merely let it go. When he thought about it, he'd not been sure how he'd react to her. But now that she was here, he didn't feel charitable. Not, anyway, as much as he thought he might.

She'd earned this discomfort. Drake glanced at Jharak without moving his head. His father was watching both his son and his wife.

Brennan and Iris were decidedly neutral. That wasn't like Iris at all. *Ah.* She didn't forgive easily either, Drake remembered.

Nerida spoke again. "Will you please, Drake, my son, accept my apology, and know that I meant no harm? I know that I caused it, but it was not..." she stopped. Then began again, "I am asking for your forgiveness. I realize that I have damaged things between us, but I am asking for the chance to try and make them right." Now she met his eyes.

Drake could see the fear and the pride that was a part of his mother at war with one another in her eyes. Did he want to forgive her? In looking at the rest of his family, they were quiet. They were allowing Drake to make the decision. For his noisy, opinionated family to shut it meant that they supported him.

Even against his mother, if he wished. It was nearly overwhelming. He turned away. He needed a moment to gather his thoughts.

"Drake—" Nerida began.

He held up a hand. The room went silent once more.

Finally, he thought he might be able to speak coherently. He faced Nerida, not looking at anyone else. "Mother, your words did damage. You might as well have slashed me with a blade."

Nerida made a gasping noise, but other than covering her mouth, she was still.

"I have wrestled with how to manage settling accounts with you. I still have no good answer. The things you said, they are reminiscent of all the shameful whispers I endured growing up. To hear them from my mother is difficult to forgive. I am unsure that I will be able to."

Nerida stood frozen.

"But I am willing to try. I will ask that you behave as though nothing is wrong with us. It's important for this Realm to see that the new king has the backing of the Fae King and Queen." He smiled. Not as large or open of a smile that Jharak had gotten, but it was genuine.

"May I embrace you?" She asked in a small, formal voice.

He nodded and came towards her with his arms open. She wrapped her arms around him, and if he wasn't mistaken, was making sniffing noises. He let her.

Drake didn't like fighting with his mother. This might never be right, not as it had been. But it was a start, and she had made the overture. That alone told him how much she felt that she had made a mistake. Nerida never made the first move.

She let go of him and rested her hand on his cheek. "I am very proud of you. I shall take care that my pride as a mother is all that is seen."

Iris, standing behind Nerida, made a noise that was at best, disbelieving. Nerida didn't acknowledge it.

"Thank you, Mother. That would be appropriate." Drake felt off kilter, speaking so formally. It wasn't how he spoke to Nerida. But it was the best he could do.

Nerida's eyes looked shiny, and she looked to Jharak. He smiled at her. Jharak took his wife's hand and clapped Drake on the shoulder.

"That is all that can be asked, Drake. Thank you. Now, what needs to be addressed before the coronation? We wanted to be here so that any last minute items might be handled."

Drake thought Jharak's being here might make things more full of last minute items to be handled, but he didn't say so. It was good that his family thought of him.

As though he'd been listening at the door, Treven came in, followed by kitchen maids carrying trays. As Drake realized that there was nowhere for everyone to sit, footmen came in and set up a long table and two benches. A single chair was brought in and placed at the head of the table. The footmen finished by covering the table with a cloth and set the table with a precision Drake wouldn't have expected.

The chair is for me, Drake thought with a start.

As the maids were serving the food, Treven said, "Sire, if you and your guests would care to sit?"

Drake hid his smile. This was a good choice of a manservant. His former awe disappeared in the wake of the responsibilities of his station.

Drake waited as the ladies were seated, and then he took the chair. Brennan and Jharak sat. The maids served the meal in silence, overseen by Trevan.

When everyone was served Trevan spoke. "Sire, please ring if you need me." He bowed and left the room.

The silence lasted until after the door had closed.

"Wow! How'd you get him trained and together so fast?" Iris asked.

"Well, he's not a goblin, for one," Drake said. He knew how the goblins could be at times.

"We need a guy like that," Iris said to Brennan, looking at the closed door.

"You'd break the hearts of your kitchen staff," Drake said, taking a bite. "You know that, don't you?"

With a last longing look at the door, Iris sighed and began eating. "You're right. We would."

"I like our staff," Brennan said. "They are—"

"Unique," Iris finished with a laugh.

That made them both laugh.

"Where's Aine?" Iris asked.

Drake rolled his eyes. "Either organizing something or down with the dragons."

"Have you seen them again?" Brennan asked.

"Yes, and I would like to have some time to speak with you on them later. But you asked where she was, and I'm giving you the best guess." Drake was annoyed she wasn't here.

"Well, we shall see her later, won't we?" Iris asked.

"She had planned on it, as far as I know," Drake shrugged.

"Your kitchens are doing well," Jharak said, holding up a piece of bread and changing the subject. "Have you gotten the market running?"

"Father, the cooks tell me there hasn't been a market for as long as they could remember," Drake said, still startled by the fact.

Nerida sniffed, sounding much like her old self. "Eilor never seemed to care that the ladies of his Realm had to spirit away dressmakers and all those who provided the necessities from others to stay clothed."

Drake frowned. "The courtiers do not seem to be shabbily dressed, Mother."

She shook her head. "They are not. But the ladies of the Dragon Realm are resourceful. They've had to be."

"That might have been nice to know," Drake said, looking from Jharak to Nerida. How had Jharak not known this?

"I have been remiss. How did I not know this, my dear?" Jharak asked.

Nerida frowned at him, but it was not a frown of anger. "Because you men don't think of such things. The women handle the households. I could have told you if—"

"If we'd all been speaking," Iris interrupted. She focused on her food.

An awkward silence descended over the table.

Nerida started to say something, but Iris cut her off again.

"I am not going to pretend, when it's just family, that there was no rift. It's stupid. There was a rift. You weren't talking to anyone." Iris looked up, and around at everyone. "No sense in pretending something didn't happen. I'm not passing judgment, either, Nerida. You have owned your mess, and I believe you're trying to make things better. But I don't lie, or cover the truth with a pretty kind of lie. She's right, too," Iris added.

"While it's the staff who carries things out, they come to the lady of the house for direction and management. And you guys can just kill something and make pants, so your needs aren't the same," she finished.

Drake thought she sounded disgusted. He knew she preferred her human trousers more than most of her fae clothing. He couldn't help smiling.

To his surprise, Nerida wasn't ready to blast Iris' hair off. Instead, she gave her daughter-in-law a look that might almost be termed 'fond.'

"So what have you done about it?" Jharak asked

Drake was grateful for the return to non-emotional matters. "We have set things in motion to begin a regular, weekly market," he said and gave the details.

Normal conversation followed. He'd completely forgotten about holding Court until Trevan returned.

"Sire," he bowed. "The guests are beginning to arrive."

"Oh, hell," Drake said. "I'd forgotten. See that everyone is properly seated, or given refreshment, or whatever is done for those attending, Trevan. We shall be down shortly."

"Please ring for me, sire. I would ensure you are properly announced," Trevan gave him a look that was nearly stern.

As he left, Drake wondered had he just been lectured by his manservant? Trevan was going to be perfect for him. He preferred it when someone else worried about the details.

"Announced for what?" Nerida asked.

"I'm delighted that you all showed up," Drake grinned at everyone. "You're going to be part of the first Court I hold. It will either go off well or be a spectacular disaster. I only sent out invitations today and alerted the staff at the same time. I am sure my name is the subject of curses downstairs."

"They'll think you're as mad as Eilor," Brennan smirked.

Drake shrugged. "In all honesty, I couldn't be any worse. The man is—was a complete menace. Speaking of which, I need a steward. And maybe a recommendation for a mage. And a gardener. And..." he threw up his hands. "But at least I'm not skulking all over the castle, dragging the Realm to ruin. I'll need to know where I can sell some jewels, as well." He thought of the hoard he and Aine found in Ailla's rooms. Maybe that would be enough to start taming the gardens?

Jharak stared for a moment, and then laughed, a roaring laugh that made him lean back in his chair. When he could speak, he said, "You're going to be fine, Drake. What's the purpose of tonight? You're going to see them all shortly."

Drake leaned his head to the side. "I've thought

since we talked about the market. I decided that I couldn't take this on alone because I would probably die before I got rid of all the things that need addressing here. So I thought that bringing in the courtiers, showing them the new king, and asking for help would be the best thing. It also," he held up a hand, "Gives me the chance to see who is not helpful."

"Nicely done," Jharak responded. "We'll have time to talk after the coronation."

"How long are you staying?"

"Are you ready to boot us?" Iris asked with a laugh.

"You will probably be on my *please leave* list shortly," Drake teased. "No, not at all. I just need to let the staff know. They are excited that you're here, and while I don't know why, they are eager to get a look at you, ladyship. I think the excitement may not be justified," he rolled his eyes in mock dismay.

"You wouldn't even have the slightest clue," Iris said, unfazed. "So let's get this show on the road, then."

Drake caught Brennan's eye. "She's all yours," he said, with the air of one who escaped.

Brennan smiled in a way that could only be called smug. "Indeed she is."

17

AINE

I resisted the urge to drag Taranath along by the arm.

"My lady, we do have a lot of things to do—" he protested.

"Yes, and taking advantage of when Fangorn is talkative is one of them. We're almost there. Don't be shocked," I added.

"Why?"

"Because he's big, and...well," I looked over at Taranath. "He's a dragon."

"I am honored that you chose me. Please don't think otherwise," he said.

"I know, I know," I said as we reached the bottom of the stairs. "We do have a lot to do. But I don't think it's a good idea to ignore the request to speak.

You know magic, and so does Fangorn. This may help us."

I didn't specify who 'us' was. I wanted to see if I could help Fangorn and the other dragons. And Drake. And myself. And the Realm. But my priorities were maybe a bit different than anyone else's.

Taranath gave me a penetrating glance. I felt as though he could see within me. I didn't like it, but I saw no other way. I knew, although I didn't know how I knew, that nothing in the Realm would be right if we didn't make things right with the dragons.

"All right. Are you ready?" I asked.

He nodded. I saw something in his face—he was excited. Good. I wanted others to feel positive about the dragons.

Thank you, daughter.

The torches increased the light. More than normal, I noticed. That must be Fangorn.

He was right next to the door of his cage. I turned, wanting to introduce Taranath, but he'd stopped and was staring at one of the sleeping dragons.

"It's true," he said quietly.

"Yes, it is. Did you think this was all a lie?"

Slowly, Taranath shook his head. "You hear that there are dragons, but when so few have seen them, much of what one hears becomes rumor, conjecture." He faced me. "I am sorry, I am dithering."

"Come and meet Fangorn," I said, smiling.

Taranath stood at my shoulder, and I looked back at Fangorn. There was an air of amusement around him, although I couldn't be sure. He was in dragon form.

"Taranath, this is Fangorn, who is the only one of the dragons awake. He has been awake for many years, so many he is unsure of the exact number. He is also a shifter, and capable of shifting to fae form."

Taranath bowed at the waist. "My lord Fangorn, it is a privilege to meet you."

I could tell that the formality pleased Fangorn. He inclined his head gracefully as Taranath stood.

You're acting like this is a state visit, I thought.

Isn't it? He asked.

"I am pleased you are willing to meet me. My daughter Aine tells me we have many things to speak of."

"I believe we do," Taranath said, stepping closer. "The magic is almost alive within this cavern. Is that all you?"

Nothing like jumping right in. I crossed my arms. No need for me to interrupt.

Fangorn shrugged. "I cannot tell. We are a collective, you understand. I was speaking to Aine about this recently. When they wake, my brethren will know all that has passed here, in spite of the fact that they have been asleep for it. They will know of my dealings with Eilor, my lost children, and of where matters stand. There is always awareness, although I cannot say how long it may take for them to be fully present."

"I am sorry that you find yourself here," Taranath said.

"Are you? We did a fine job of nearly destroying the entire Realm," Fangorn said in a dry tone.

Now it was Taranath's turn to shrug. "Does that signify that you then spend thousands of years in a cage, in an a state of existence?"

"Should we have been put to death?"

"Should you have?" Taranath didn't hold back either.

I hadn't spent much time with the mage. I knew that Drake, Iris, and Brennan thought highly of him. Now I could begin to see why. He was quiet, but there was a strength in him that reminded me of a strong blade.

Fangorn hadn't been expecting that. I saw his green eyes widen.

"I do not know. I've had a long time to consider," the eyes narrowed. "I don't know if it would be better. I would have spared my mates, and my children that came after captivity, yes. They suffered and then died needlessly for a man who deserves a slow and painful death. But then, that would mean no Aine, and I find her to be one of the positive things that come from my long years of pain."

I could feel the tears prick at my eyes, and my throat tighten. I didn't know if Taranath could hear it, but I could feel the years of suffering in his words.

I am sorry, Fangorn said. *That is part of our collective, to feel what others have felt. I would spare you, but I cannot.*

I shook my head. *It's all right. There is no reason to be dishonest about the past.*

Taranath glanced between us. "Do you communicate silently?"

"You know about that?"

"I have read that silent communication was one of the things that made the dragons so formidable," Taranath said.

"It did," Fangorn answered. "I make you a promise, Mage. If you are able to find a way to open the doors, if the new king is not, I will allow you to question and study me."

"Why?" I asked before I could help myself.

"Because after so many years in this environment, I am unsure of what I can do, what my abilities are. Dragons are slow to adapt, but all things change, even us. I would know what changes I must live with."

Taranath looked Fangorn up and down. "Are any of the others shifters?"

"No. That is my gift alone."

"Why do you think the cages will not open?" Taranath shifted the conversation.

It didn't seem like him to be so abrupt. I snuck a look at Fangorn. He didn't seem bothered. I forgot, sometimes, how dragons were different when it came to speaking. Taranath must have realized that.

"Eilor told me that until he died, they would never open." The anger and desolation came through the simple statement.

Taranath walked closer, running a hand along the bars of Fangorn's cage. Then he went past it and did the same along the other five cages. He crossed the cavern, touching the bars of all the cages until he made his way back to us.

Fangorn and I watched, not speaking, not even silently.

When Taranath had completed his circle, he stopped between me and the cage. "The magic spells that keep the doors locked are different on each cage," he said. "They are old, very old spells. Some are more recent, specifically around your cell, My lord," He looked up at Fangorn. "I believe most of those sleeping are guarded by the original spells that were placed on them. You, and the cages on either side of you have the most recent spells." He tapped his chin, thinking.

"They are more entwined with this castle, with the Realm. I cannot untangle them with only a simple pass. But I do not feel that these spells are tied to any one person. Would you like me to try and open your cage?"

I started. I didn't think that Drake would be happy because he was worried. But—I saw Fangorn's eyes glow.

Will you promise me that you don't get overwhelmed with freedom, should it come? I asked.

He growled, and I had no idea if that was a 'yes' or a 'no.'

"Be careful, Mage. I place no trust in the spells of Eilor to leave you unscathed."

Taranath nodded, and pulling stones from a pouch at his belt; he held his hands out to the bars. He didn't speak, but I could tell that he was casting a spell. The stones in his hand glowed a hot white, the circle of light getting bigger around his hands until I couldn't see them any longer.

The cavern rumbled.

The bars in front of Fangorn rattled. I'd never heard any of them rattle before. Fangorn shuffled back.

Taranath staggered backward as the stones, still surrounded by light, flew out of his hands. One shot up towards the ceiling, and the other one flew in front of me. As they hit the ground, the glow disappeared.

"Taranath! Are you all right?" I hurried to him. Drake—and Brennan—would be seriously displeased if I harmed this man, or rather, allowed him to be harmed. Not that I wanted to see him hurt. I liked him.

He held up a hand, bending over a little. "I am fine, merely winded, Lady Aine. The spells that protect the doors are strong. There is no doubt." He set his hands on his knees, breathing heavily.

After a moment, he stood. "I am sorry if I alarmed you, my lady. I wasn't expecting the resistance I encountered. You are correct, My lord. The spells will not be broken, at this time. It's as though there is a barrier I cannot cross."

I could feel Fangorn's sadness at these words.

"I am not surprised, Mage. Eilor, while he made many mistakes, was thorough in his malice."

"Isn't he dead?" Taranath looked to me.

"All the kings involved believe he is. I am not so sure," I answered him.

"I wonder..." Taranath pursed his lips. "I wonder if it is Eilor or the Dragon King who commands this."

"You have made the same leap I did, Mage. I do not know. Eilor did not say. No doubt that was a deliberate choice on his part," Fangorn said.

"He was an evil man," I said. I couldn't stop the anger from coming out.

"He is an evil man," Fangorn corrected.

"There you have it," I said. "We can't agree on whether he's dead or alive. I want to believe it, but I am afraid that if I do, I'll be wrong."

"It is better to assume the worst and be prepared," Taranath said. "Although my understanding is that a body with the clothing that Eilor wore was found. I believe that some items that he carried were also found."

I knew that Taranath had inspected the ring. He knew I knew. Why wasn't he admitting it?

Loyalty to his king. He is a good man, this mage.

Too many alliances to keep track off, I grumbled. *Aren't we all on the same side?*

Fangorn snorted. A puff of smoke wafted up from his nostrils, and I saw that Taranath watched it just as I did. Even now, it was somewhat unreal to be chatting with a dragon.

"When I am free, when the doors open for me and those with me, then I will believe he is gone. Until then, I do not. No matter what is found," Fangorn said.

"I am unable to break the spell at this time," Taranath said. "But I will keep working. The Lady Aine gave me a massive pile of papers and notes from Eilor's rooms. Perhaps there is something there that could be of help. I must ask, however," his lips tightened, "What do you plan to do once free, Lord Fangorn? The world is, as you have mentioned, not the world you once knew."

I could see why everyone liked Taranath so much. He was kind, polite, and considerate. I could also see why Drake wanted to steal him from his brother. Nothing he'd done had been wrong. He was very much an asset, and he was magically skilled as well.

Fangorn sighed. "I do not know, Mage. I find the thought troubling. I will no doubt need to meet with the Fae King, who is one of those who had me placed here. I do not know if I will be able to put aside my anger. While I understand that to the victor goes the spoils, I do not understand why there was no one who insisted that Eilor provide an accounting of his stewardship of us. This," a wave around the cavern, "Would have been discovered. But it wasn't. No one wanted to face that there were creatures who might be in need! So it was assumed that Eilor was a good man, an honorable man, and we were left at his mercy! With no one to stop him in whatever he chose to do!" He got up, restless. He stomped to the back of the cage.

Taranath and I exchanged glances.

"That was not my intention, my lady," he said. "I am sorry."

"It's all right," I said. "Fangorn is correct, and he's entitled to be angry."

"I am," Fangorn said. He'd come back and heard my last statement. "As are you, daughter. Both of us," He turned his head to Taranath, "Learned in our dealings with Eilor that one does not show emotion, or anger, or hurt, or anything that might bring any further attention to ourselves. To be able to express myself is a luxury that I have not had for many years. I will no longer be silent."

"Nor should you be," I said. "I understand, Grandfather. I do not think those who we deal with now are lacking in understanding or empathy," I added.

Fangorn stared at me. I couldn't read his expression.

"I hope you are right," he said. Without another word, he turned and moved to the back of his cage.

Clearly, this meeting was finished. I gave Taranath a slight shrug. "I'm sorry. This is difficult for him."

"Thank you for seeing me, My lord," Taranath spoke loudly, and then he turned and moved to the stairs.

"I shall see you tomorrow, Grandfather," I said, letting my hand brush against the bars in front of me. I wanted to say more, but I didn't know what to say.

Enjoy the day, daughter. No one but me owns my past.

I followed Taranath up the steps. We didn't speak; both lost in our thoughts. As I opened the door and led him out of the corridor, I took care, as I always did, to lock the door behind me.

"Thank you for coming with me." I felt awkward with the way things had ended.

He smiled. "Thank you for trusting me. He is truly an amazing being. But I understand his fear, and yours. I also understand the concerns of my king. This is a complex situation, my lady. I will put my thoughts towards a solution that will bring peace to as many as it can."

"Thank you," I said again.

"Now, I would suggest that you go and ready yourself for Lord Drake's Court tonight. I know that his family has arrived. I believe," his eyebrows went up, "That the Fae Queen is here with them."

"Really?" I asked. I was surprised. I'd not seen her since the night when Cian and Ailla were killed. She was very upset with everyone there. Wrongly, in my opinion, but no one had asked.

Taranath nodded. "Yes. They were having dinner in the King's chambers. So I heard before I joined you. I am sure you have time to prepare yourself. I know Drake would like you with him," he finished.

"You'll be there as well?" I asked.

"Of course. I need to talk with my king if I am going

to be here longer. I have duties at the Goblin Castle that I am not tending to."

"I'm glad you're here," I said. "You're right. I'd better go and tidy." I looked down. While I wore a gown, I was dusty, and there were smudges on the gown itself. I wasn't used to wearing finery. Which meant that my clothing suffered.

I hurried to my rooms, debating what I would wear. This was an important meeting. It would allow Drake to set his footing with his court. I didn't want to do anything or call attention to myself in any manner that would derail his plans for the evening.

When I reached my rooms, the first thing I saw was the journals, stacked up and sitting on the table near my bed. When had Drake decided to return them to me? I looked again. No. They weren't there. He hadn't returned them. I was seeing things, letting fear and worry cloud my vision.

No one but me owns my past. Fangorn's words drifted through my head. He was right. He was often right.

"Oh, shut it," I said crossly. I took off my wrinkled gown and threw it on my bedside table. Where the journals had once resided. Now they were with Drake. I looked again. They weren't there. The dress floated down over the table. At least I didn't need to look at where they'd been.

My past. I can cover it if I want to.

18

DRAKE

*H*e stood with the rest of his family. Where was Taranath? Where was Aine?

As if called, Taranath glided towards them. When he came to Drake, he stopped and bowed. "My apologies, My lord. I was preoccupied earlier."

"With Aine?" Drake asked.

Taranath stood up and nodded. "Yes. She had some concerns she wished to discuss."

Drake waited, but Taranath didn't say anything else.

"Well, I'm glad you were able to help her. Is she on her way as well?"

"As far as I know."

To think he'd laughed quietly when Brennan was

irritated at the mannerisms of the mage. Turnabout was not pleasant at this point.

"Do we need to wait for her?" Nerida asked.

Drake shot her a glance. "Yes, Mother, we do. I go out united or not at all." The words came before he could even think twice about them.

Nerida looked as though she wanted to reply, and Jharak raised his eyebrows, but no one said a thing.

Drake turned as he heard the footsteps of someone running. A moment later, Aine appeared.

"I am sorry—oh, no! Have I kept you waiting?"

"Yes, but it's all right. It doesn't hurt the rest of the Court to wait," Drake said. He couldn't help it. He smiled at her, surprised at how relieved he felt to have her there.

"Well, let's get this circus underway," Iris said.

Everyone turned to look at her.

"What? Is it not a circus? Please," Iris rolled her eyes.

"Drake, why don't you lead the way? We'll follow you," Brennan said.

Drake smiled at his brother. He took a breath and walked into the hall, where he could hear the murmur of a large crowd of people. There was no reason to be nervous. There was—

"Usurper!" The voice, a male voice, rang out as soon as Drake entered the hall.

He'd deliberately not placed any throne in the hall. There was a small dais, to help people in the crowd to see better, but there was merely a row of chairs upon it, all the same, none more or less than the rest.

He sighed.

The whispers raced through the crowd. Drake knew at that moment that this would be where he won or lost this Realm.

He held up a hand. The whispers died down.

Drake walked towards the chair closest to the middle and faced all the people waiting.

"I would ask you all, do you wish to return to the Dragon Realm as it was? Before you answer, think carefully. I know," he made himself take the time to look intently at all the people he could, "There are those among you who have prospered with the preoccupation of your former king. But if you are honest, would you say that your Realm has prospered? That there is an air of contentment in this Realm? I know I am but lately from the Goblin Realm," Drake smiled as a hum of laughter greeted those remarks.

"And while there are those who would disparage my former home, I can tell you that the goblins are, for the most part, happy, content, and willing to do their part for the Realm, rather than just their family, or their interests. Can you say the same?"

After the time he'd spent with the cooks alone, and

the fired steward, he knew this wasn't true. Those who could take were taking, and the rest were scrabbling for what was left. He was hoping that the latter would feel empowered.

"Not to mention, is the Fae King to leave this Realm with no one at the helm, no one to guide the Dragon Realm?"

Silence greeted his question. Drake could see people in the crowd whispering, but before anyone could answer, Jharak stepped forward.

"As the Fae King and the ruler of all the Realms, I did not take this step lightly. I will share with you the reason I decided as I did. I am sure that many of you," Jharak smiled at a woman who was staring at him, "Have heard of the battle that lately occurred in my Castle. Yes?" His question brought a wave of assent from the crowd.

"I have deliberately withheld the information, wanting to tell this Realm first what happened. Ailla, your princess, and the man you knew as Kelan, attacked me, the Queen," he indicated Nerida, "And the Goblin King and Queen. His intent was to kill all of us. What you might not know is that Kelan was once my son, Cian." Jharak let his head drop.

Drake didn't think the sadness anything other than genuine. Nor did he think that Nerida's lip trembling an act.

The crowd gave up whispering at that point. Jharak held up a hand. "I know. I—we—thought him long dead. But he was not. Unfortunately, the boy we lost was truly lost. Kelan—Cian—was a son in name only." Jharak's eyes narrowed. "He was insane. Something happened during the years that he spent here in the Dragon Realm. I would guess that many of you knew him, or had some interaction with him?"

The noise stilled at the question. Drake could see that no one wanted to admit it.

Jharak saw it too. "I gather, from what I have since learned, that he spent most of his time with Eilor. Whatever Kelan was, in the end, was due to the influence of that man. Is that the sort of man you would still wish for your king? A man who would hide a child from grieving parents, and turn him into someone unrecognizable?" Jharak took a breath. "While Kelan and Ailla had a plan that was focused on them alone, I know that Eilor knew of it. Is that the sort of man you still wish for? You, who shouted at my son Drake as we entered? Is that what you miss? A man who was so focused on harming other that he has allowed the Realm he was entrusted with to slide into disrepair?" Jharak stepped forward.

Drake knew that he had to do this on his own, although he appreciated what Jharak said. He put a hand on his father's arm and stepped in front of him.

"I know from speaking with the staff here that no one can easily acquire goods or even food. We are working now on making daily life easier. When was the last time anyone did that for you? This is not a rhetorical question. I want to know."

Drake knew that no one would be able to answer without lying. The whispers died down as everyone looked to see if the person who'd shouted when he'd entered would speak up.

He opened his mouth to move on when a man stepped out from the crowd into an open space.

"You are not the king, and no ceremony or push by your father will change that," the man said, his voice loud and strong.

"Who are you?" Drake asked.

"Niles!" Aine hissed behind him. "Be careful!"

"So you are the man who stood at the hand of the king," Drake said.

Niles crossed his arms. "I am," he said.

"You speak for the former king?" Drake continued.

"I would not dare, but you are not he, nor is this the Realm of any other than King Eilor," Niles said, not looking anywhere but at Drake.

"Then perhaps you can answer why I have found that people are going hungry, and struggle to get basic goods for their families," Drake said, stepping down from the dais. "I am appalled that this Realm seems to lack in so many of the basic items that the rest of the Realms take for granted. I have seen, as you no doubt have, from the treasurer, that the former king took in his yearly taxes from the Realm. Where are they?" He crossed his arms and glared back.

"I do not know," Niles said. "That is not my purview."

"What is your responsibility, exactly?" Drake continued to walk towards the man. He felt, rather than saw, the other members of the Court move away as he came near. *Good,* he thought. *Let them see me as I am. A warrior. Unafraid.* This was the sort of thing he felt comfortable in.

But he forced himself not to rest his hand on the pommel of his sword. He didn't want to present a threat until he needed to. Still, he was glad he'd buckled it on before coming into the hall tonight.

"One would think the man at the hand of the king would be concerned, as would the king, for the well-being of the Realm?" Drake asked, looking around at the faces of the courtiers. "Does that seem reasonable?"

He was encouraged to see a few nods. He noted that people glanced fearfully at Niles. "Has this man been a good steward for you? Because I can tell you that I have dismissed the man who held that post for the castle. He was cheating the Realm to line his own pockets!" He raised his brows, hoping that the expression he'd seen on Jharak's face so many times in the past would work here. "Were you aware of that, Niles?"

He could tell the man was surprised that Drake knew his name.

"I—" Niles began.

He didn't get very far. A voice rang out from behind where Drake stood.

"You can say nothing, Niles," Aine sneered. "I have seen, many times, Niles extort payment from many here! And yet, none of you will speak! Do you not wonder why, My lord Drake?"

Drake turned slightly so that he could see her. He wanted to see where she was heading with her actions. This was not like her. But he also didn't want to take his eyes off Niles.

"Now that you bring it to my attention, yes. I do. Do you have an answer, my lady Aine?"

"Oh, I do," she said. Her face held fury as she, too, stepped off the dais and came to where Drake stood. "He threatened them. Not only with his ability to practice magic, but the threat of what the *king*," her voice sneered over the word, "Might do. People had no choice to give over whatever it was Niles demanded. He threatened wives, children, family. Nothing was sacred!"

"You lie!" Niles roared. "How dare you speak to me so?" His hands fumbled at a pouch at his waist.

Things happened so quickly Drake nearly didn't see it. He saw Niles, reaching for what he guessed were stones. Before Niles could reach into his pouch, Aine had shouted something, and green light flew from her hands. Just as the spell hit Niles, a pink and then a white flare shot from the crowd. Drake couldn't tell where—or who—it had come from.

The man flew backward, with people in the crowd screaming as they dove to get out of the way. One woman wasn't so lucky, and Niles slammed into her as he flew towards the back of the hall.

Drake didn't have time to tend to her. As quickly as he fell, Niles stood. That was a strong man, Drake thought.

Niles shouted something that Drake couldn't understand, and a black mist surrounded him. He felt people come up behind him and saw Iris and Taranath join Aine, all with hands outstretched.

The black mist swirled, making all who encountered it cough and double over.

"Move!" Drake shouted, and he reached for the woman closest to him, pulling her back towards the dais. He was pleased to see the three who stood with him do the same, and people scrambled back.

The hall went silent as everyone watched the mist.

It swirled up, filling the space towards the ceiling. Drake watched it and then fell back as the mist exploded in a burst of flame that rained down.

The hall was in chaos.

Taranath raised his hands, and a white mist appeared and snuffed out the flames.

Drake spoke to the woman he'd pulled away. "Are you all right?"

She nodded, her movements shaky.

He patted her arm, and then looked around. Raising his arms, he yelled, "Be still!"

His voice rang out in the hall, and people listened. Drake was surprised, frankly.

"Is anyone hurt?" Quietly he said to Taranath, "Find him."

Taranath nodded, and Iris and Aine followed him before anyone could stop them.

Drake hadn't meant for the women to go with the mage, and he shot Brennan an apologetic look. There was no stopping Iris when she was determined, so he figured he couldn't be held fully responsible. He didn't want to be shouting at his family in front of the entire Dragon Court. Better to let the women look like leaders in their own right.

Brennan and Jharak, along with Nerida and the mages that had been working with Taranath went through the crowd, making sure that any small hurts or injuries were addressed. It was done faster than Drake thought it would be, and his parents joined him.

"I believe we've seen all the people who suffered any hurt," Brennan said. "But I am wondering where my wife and my mage are." His brows furrowed, a sure sign of worry.

"Come on," Drake said. "They are with Taranath, and that is the best we can do. The ladies need to fend for themselves. Ease up," he clapped Brennan on the shoulder, "Your bride is not a fair maiden with no skills. We need to tend to matters here, and then we will search out the rat."

Brennan stood, staring at the door where Taranath, Iris, and Aine had left at the other end of the hall.

"Bren," Drake said, stopping. "We must present a united front. You and I must show that we feel the women of our family," he realized that he was including Aine in that, and he found that he didn't mind a bit, "Are capable on their own."

"Drake is right," Jharak said.

"There is no doubt that both of them can hold their own," Nerida said grudgingly.

Drake could see that everyone was watching them. He needed to pull this evening back together and give people time to speak to him. To show them that he would listen, and a little thing like a crazed former supporter of Eilor would only set the schedule off a bit. That this was, as Iris put it, no big deal.

A smile cracked Brennan's worried expression. It didn't travel to his eyes, but it was a start. "She can, can't she?"

"Yes," Drake said. He was worried, but he meant every word. His sister-in-law was fearsome, and her time in the Goblin Realm had only made her more so. "Come, brother. I'm the one who needs your lordship's help at the moment," he grinned.

It worked. Brennan smiled more broadly, and this time, Drake was glad to see, it reached his eyes.

"Lead on, My lord King," Brennan said mockingly.

Drake cast a last glance at the back of the hall. He hoped that they found Niles.

Preferably dead.

19

AINE

I ran alongside Taranath and Iris, who, for being pregnant, was fast.

"Did you see where he went through the mist?" I asked, hoping that someone had. "I didn't."

"That was the point of the spell, my lady," Taranath said. "Where would he hide?" He stopped so abruptly I nearly ran into him.

I had to think about it. "The only times I saw him were in Eilor's—"

"His rooms?" Iris asked.

I shook my head. "No, his workroom. That was separate."

"Where did Niles have rooms?"

I thought some more. "I don't know. I'm sorry," I

said. I'd lived here my entire life, and I didn't know where the slinking weasel lived.

"Wait," Taranath said. "Let us see if we can see him."

"How?" Iris asked.

"I need you to both take my hands and concentrate on helping me see. I can show you the spell later, but I need your help now." Taranath held out his hands.

I took his hand, as did Iris. He closed his eyes, and I could feel the magic running through him as clearly as the stream in the woods behind the castle. I hadn't realized how much magic Taranath was capable of, in spite of how much I'd seen him do.

Beads of sweat formed along his hairline as he concentrated, and my hand grew sweaty in his grip.

With an explosive breath, he let go of both of our hands. "He conceals himself. He is strong. Did he work with the mages here?"

I shook my head. "No. He and Eilor worked together, and I didn't get to see much of it. The mages —" I shook my head again. "I felt sorry for them. Eilor drew from them, but didn't allow them to do much."

"We will need to see if we can find him without magic," Taranath said. "Sadly, I am unable to see him. Let us go to the workroom. Do you know where it is?" He asked me.

"You haven't been in them?" I couldn't hold back my surprise. "None of the mages took you there?"

"Should they have?"

"I don't know," I said. "I guess I just thought that Eilor would have—"

"I think we can agree that we shouldn't assume anything about that bastard," Iris said, her voice grimmer than I'd ever heard. "This damn family," she muttered.

I remembered her punching Ailla in the nose. She had as much reason as I did to hate them. "I agree," I said, surprising myself and placing a hand on her arm as we walked. "They can't be dead soon enough," I added.

She grinned at me. "I never thought I was so bloodthirsty, but I don't give a damn if they die," she said. "I hope Eilor is dead, but I wasn't sure. Now I'm even less sure." She flapped a hand as I opened my mouth. "I know they saw him, but did you hear that guy Niles? He didn't sound like he believed Eilor was dead! Sheesh, I'd be suspicious that that bitch Ailla was still here if I hadn't seen her die myself," Iris huffed in frustration.

"Are you feeling all right?" I asked. I hoped that Brennan wouldn't be angry that we hadn't sent her back. She was new to magic, but everything I'd seen said that she was skilled.

Iris waved a hand. "I'm fine. I just puff like a train sometimes."

"What's a train?" I asked.

"Never mind," she said. "I'm fine. That's what matters."

"Which way, Lady Aine?" Taranath asked, calling us back to order.

"This way," I answered, focusing. Would he really have come back here? I didn't think so, but it was worth a look.

Suddenly, a burst of flame shot out from what looked like a wall. Then Niles stepped out of it, hands outstretched.

"Long live the king!" He shouted.

That struck me as odd, but I didn't have time to think about it.

As one, Taranath, Iris, and I all shot spells at him. I could tell that he wasn't expecting anything from Iris or me.

That was always one of his weaknesses. Niles hated women—hated anyone other than Eilor. He even hated Ailla, but I didn't consider that a major defect. It was his one moment of common sense, in my opinion.

The spells hit Niles one after the other. I sent one that was meant to stop him. He did, in fact stop, and pretty abruptly. His body jerked as the spells struck him. His hands were outstretched, and the fingers uncurled. Several stones fell from each hand. His mouth opened and closed, and then silently, as though the corridor itself held its breath, he fell.

Oh, no. I hadn't meant to kill him. Or had I?

Iris spoke first. "That's it?" She asked.

"It would seem so, my lady," Taranath said. He walked closer to the body.

Not too close, I noted.

Then a small thread of light drifted from Taranath's hands and moved towards Niles' body. It enveloped him in a soft blue glow.

"What are you doing?" I asked.

"I'm making sure he's dead," Taranath said without looking at me.

No one spoke as the light moved all over Niles. After what seemed an eternity, the light disappeared, and Taranath turned to us.

"He is gone, my ladies. There is no life left in him, and no trickery or magic associated with him in any fashion any longer."

I stared at the body. Niles was dead. I hadn't been able to see Eilor, and I really would have liked to.

"You're sure?" I asked. I didn't recognize my voice. Had I been part of killing him? Did I care?

"I am," Taranath said.

I walked around him and stood looking down at the body. Niles' head lolled to the side. His mouth had fallen slightly open, and he looked like he'd gone to sleep.

"Sleep forever in torment, you miserable creature," I said.

Then I drew back my foot and kicked him in the face.

I'd forgotten that I was wearing soft slippers, rather than the boots I usually wore.

"OW!" I pulled my foot back and bent down to massage the toes. That hurt. A lot. It figured. The one time I indulged in being nasty, I got hurt.

"Are you all right?" Iris came toward me, putting a hand on my arm.

I shook my head. "He deserves worse, but I don't need to hurt myself any further on his behalf."

"No, you don't," she said, putting her arm around me.

Normally, that sort of touch would make me want to move away, as quickly as possible. But Iris felt comfortable, and I knew she meant well. So I forced myself not to shudder, or show any negative reaction. I didn't want to hurt her feelings.

Taranath looked around. "I'm surprised there isn't a guard that has come searching for you, my lady," he looked at Iris. "The King being as concerned as he is."

"Perhaps he just knows I'll be fine. You know, since I'm with you?" Iris asked him.

They looked at one another, and then Iris laughed.

"Yeah, that's probably a big old nope on that kind of assumption. We should go back, let them know only the person who needs to be is dead."

I nodded and followed them as they went back in the direction of the hall. I found that my throat felt unreasonably tight. I had helped to kill a man tonight.

We made our way back to the hall with me in the lead. I had to; once Iris tried to take us down the wrong corridor. Once there, Drake was still speaking, talking back and forth with the court. The three of us stopped, listening.

He was addressing the lack of a market and the fact that he was working with the castle staff and the people in the surrounding town to bring one together. I could hear the excited murmurs of the people in the room at this news. If there were people who would not appreciate the incursion into their ability to sell things quietly on the side, no one was showing any signs of disappointment. Of course, it would be foolish to do so at the moment, but that didn't mean I wasn't looking for it.

All talk ceased when those near the door noticed us.

"What news?" Drake asked loudly.

I wondered if he knew how regal he sounded. As though he were already the king.

"The traitor Niles is no more," said Iris in a loud voice.

I was glad she chose to speak. It was better that the court saw that everyone around me supporting me as part of the family. As someone who belonged.

"Very well," Drake nodded. "Guards, please go and remove him." Several men slipped out the door after a quick word from Taranath as where they would find the body.

"Let that be an example," Drake said to the crowd. "I am willing to work with you, to address your concerns, as you have seen. But if you threaten this Realm, my family, the future we are working for—you will pay the price."

A murmur ran through the hall. It wasn't quite as excited or cheerful as before. I didn't think that was a bad thing. It would go better for Drake if people knew his methods from the beginning. There would be those who challenged him, but no one could say the new king didn't warn them.

"That is enough excitement for this evening," Drake said. "Let us retire, and we will celebrate after the coronation. And then we will work together to heal the Realm."

Everyone looked around, and then quietly, somberly, filed from the hall. I could tell from the murmur that people felt all right. Perhaps not completely contented, but all right. There was a sense of hope that I'd never felt in this room—in this castle —ever.

Once it was just the family and the guards left with a nod from Drake, he looked down at the three of us. "Well, that was exciting, wasn't it?"

Silence greeted his remark and then Iris started to laugh. "Since when are you the master of the understatement? Maybe that was exciting for *you*."

"Oh, it was a bit exciting," Taranath said, one corner of his mouth curled up.

"He's dead," I said, loving the sound of the words. "Niles is dead. Eilor is dead. Ailla is dead," I could hear the quiver in my voice.

I turned away from everyone. I didn't want to make a spectacle of myself. But if I stood here for even a moment longer, I would.

All the people who made my life hell for as long as I could remember, all the people who made life unbearable—they were gone. Even with Fangorn's suspicions, even if Eilor showed up again – for the moment—he was dead. They all were.

I'd wanted this for as long as I could think

uncharitable thoughts, but now that the moment was here, I didn't know how to feel. They were gone. Dead, all of them. Dead because of the way they lived, the way they treated others—dead.

I stuffed my hand into m mouth to stop the cry from escaping and ran from the hall.

20

DRAKE

*H*e watched as Aine ran from the hall. He didn't want her to leave, but—

"What are you waiting for?" Iris turned on him ferociously. "Go after her!"

"What?" He looked down at her. "Why?"

"Oh my god," she muttered, rolling her eyes. "Guys are so...so—"

"Unaware," said his mother. "Iris is right, Drake. Go and try to be helpful."

Just who was in charge here? The day after tomorrow, it would be him, Drake thought. So why did the women in his life act like he was a small child in need of direction? And since when were Nerida and Iris in agreement about anything? Iris had recently been berating his mother.

"How can I be helpful?" He asked, throwing out his hands. "She's not—"

"Drake," Jharak said. "It's not a bad idea. Go and make sure she's all right. She'll probably go to her rooms. We'll deal with Niles and anything else that comes up."

Drake looked at him, not comprehending. Jharak thought Iris and Nerida were *right*?

"Father—"

"Aine needs a friend right now," Jharak said.

Well, that made a little more sense. He did think of her as a friend—*a friend you'd like to get closer to?* His traitorous mind inquired. *I must be going mad*, Drake thought. The voice in his head sounded sly.

Drake looked around at everyone else. Even Brennan, who he thought would be on his side, denouncing all this nonsense, was nodding.

He had no idea why everyone felt that he was the best person for this. Maybe because they didn't know what he'd done, how he'd thrown himself at her. Neither he nor Aine had said one word about it since he'd kissed her, and he found that he didn't want to. It would mean having to say that he was sorry.

And if Drake was honest with himself, even if he wouldn't admit this to anyone else—he wasn't sorry. He'd enjoyed kissing her, enjoyed it more than he'd ever enjoyed kissing any other woman. She'd driven the thoughts of Ailla and every other woman right out of his head.

It was apparent he'd get no peace until he took care of this. So he turned, and left the hall, not wanting to hear another word from anyone else. So much for being the king. As the doors of the hall shut behind him, he stopped. He could swear he heard laughter! What was that about?

Drake shook his head. There was no time to waste - he needed to catch Aine before she holed up in her room. When she'd found the journals, no one saw her for two days. She was comfortable on her own when in a hard place. He didn't want that to happen again.

He noted that people from the court were still about, and he made eye contact with them, smiling as they murmured who knew what or inclined their head. In some cases, the men bowed. He felt like an imposter, but he knew this would be his life from now on. While formality was not where he found comfort, he'd been thinking a great deal about what Jharak said regarding helping the Dragon Court to find normalcy. Allowing for formality and manners without groveling, which was what he suspected the expectation had been under Eilor, would hopefully help people move towards something resembling a normal life.

Hoping to catch up to Aine, Drake bypassed the main corridor and headed for the stairways that were for the use of the royal family. Smaller, and discreet. He hurried up the stairs, hoping to meet her before she reached her rooms.

On the floor where Aine's rooms were located, he came to the top of the stairs and jogged to her rooms.

A surge of satisfaction hit him as he saw Aine almost at her doors.

"Aine!:" Drake found he almost yelled.

She froze, then looked around. There were red blotches around her eyes, and she didn't look like the composed woman he'd grown used to seeing.

"I'm sorry that I ran out. But I am not good company at the moment, and I don't want to ruin anyone else's joy."

He stopped in front of her. "You don't feel joy that Niles is gone?"

Her brows furrowed, and he saw her shoulders hunch forward as though she could make herself invisible. That must have been how she'd managed to stay alive with Eilor as her...Well, parent all these years. The ability to keep yourself low down and unnoticed in such situations. With that one movement, Aine showed him her life. No wonder she was the way she was.

His mother might be a pain and taken far too long to come round, but she loved him. The fact that she'd made an effort to apologize—he knew Nerida loved him. That she wouldn't go out of her way to hurt him.

Aine had no such assurances. Everyone she knew had, from what she'd said, and watching her now, hurt her. Repeatedly.

Drake felt the sudden urge to rip Eilor and Niles limb from limb.

Even Ailla? His treacherous mind inquired. He knew that Ailla had gone out of her way to be unkind to Aine.

As though a door closed right in front of him, he answered without hesitation. *Even Ailla.*

He didn't miss her anymore. He didn't miss even the woman he'd thought he loved. He wished that he'd seen through her sooner than he had. That he hadn't wasted so much time mooning over a figment of his imagination. That he hadn't fallen for her lies and deception.

But that was the past. His future was right here. Now.

With...Aine?

"Can I help you with something?" She looked at him strangely, and he wondered how long she'd been waiting for him to say something.

"I...I wanted to make sure that you are all right." Drake decided that honesty, as much as he could give it, would be the best thing. Particularly as he wasn't entirely sure how he felt. "I can't understand what it must have been like to see Niles die, and I won't even pretend to understand how you feel, but I do want to make sure that you will be all right. Maybe not immediately?" He finished, feeling hesitant.

Her lips pursed, and she bit the corner of her top lip. Drake could see a sheen in her eyes that meant she might start crying again.

"I..." she stopped and bit her lip once more.

Drake felt horrid that the small movements involved in Aine's biting her lip sent a thrill of desire through him. What sort of man was he? The woman was in obvious distress! A disgusting, voyeuristic cad, that's what he—

His thought broke away as Aine flung herself at him, wrapping her arms around his middle. His arms crept around her, slowly. He was afraid that if he made a wrong move, he'd get a knife through the leg for his troubles. Even though she'd made the first move this time.

Not that he planned to kiss her! No! He'd imposed on her once before, and no matter how tempting the memory was, he wasn't going to do it again.

She just needed the shoulder—or chest, as it were —of a friend to cry on.

While Aine made no noise, her shoulders shook. Drake didn't have a lot of experience with crying women, but he was fairly certain she was crying. He let his arms rest around her, enjoying the feel of her being in his embrace voluntarily.

After a moment, he didn't know what to do. Her shoulders stopped their shaking, but Aine still had her head tucked into his chest. He didn't want to let her go; didn't want her to move.

"How can I help you?" He asked when the silence became too much for him. "I would like to help, but I don't know what to do."

At that, Aine pulled away from him. She still had her arms around him. Drake was happy to see that she didn't look ready to stab or maim him.

"There is nothing that anyone can do. To get what you wished for, after thinking it would never happen is wonderful. But it doesn't feel wonderful at the moment. I'm sure it will later..." her voice trailed away, and she looked at his chest, not willing to meet his eyes.

Then Aine looked up again. "But right now, I need to grieve. I suppose that's what I'm doing. Thank you," she said, almost shyly, looking down again. "Thank you for coming to see that I am all right."

"You're welcome," Drake said, not wanting to admit that it wasn't his idea. "Take whatever time you need. I would like to ask that you be there for the coronation, however. I want you to be with my family." He found that he did. Very much so, in fact. It wouldn't be the same if she weren't.

She met his eyes, and a faint pink stained her cheeks. "Of course I'll be there. I wouldn't miss it."

"Thank the stars. You're the only friend I have here," he said. As he spoke, he realized it was true. And that he wanted her to be more than his friend, but...he couldn't push her. Maybe, after some time, she would decide that she might care for him...he stopped his thoughts. He couldn't think like that. He had no claim on Aine.

"I doubt that, but thank you for the compliment," Aine replied. "I think I'm going to go to bed—I mean, to my room now," she said haltingly, the pink stain becoming pinker on her cheeks.

Oh, hell and damnation, Drake thought, feeling like Iris wanting to cuss. He'd embarrassed her when he kissed her, and now she was trying to back away without hurting his feelings.

He felt his cheeks get warm with shame. Everything he'd been thinking wasn't possible. Just like with Ailla, he'd become interested in someone who didn't return his interest. It didn't matter how he felt.

Because this time, he wasn't going to make a fool of himself. He wouldn't betray the trust she'd placed in him, as a friend. Or that his father had put in him, as the man about to be crowned.

No. Not this time. Not ever again. He let his arms drop from her just as she reached a hand up towards him. Just in time. He didn't want her to feel she had to physically push him away.

"Take all the time you need," Drake said, trying not to grind his teeth in disappointment. "If you need anything, let the servants know."

With a heart that felt as heavy as an anvil, Drake turned away.

In spite of all that Brennan, and Jharak, and even Iris had said, he'd always known there'd be a reckoning for his betrayal of not only his brother but all the ideals he'd held dear.

He just didn't think it would be so swift.

Or gut-wrenching.

21

AINE

*M*y hand hung in the air as I watched Drake stalk away. I'd reached up to touch his face. I wanted to kiss him again, but given his reaction to my gesture, I was grateful that I hadn't. How had I misunderstood him so thoroughly?

He'd hugged me back. When he'd kissed me before, I felt that he wanted to kiss me, and I'd wanted his kiss, his touch. When he'd asked how I was moments ago, I couldn't hold my sadness within any longer. I'd thrown myself at him, like a pathetic little girl.

Like Ailla.

A red haze crossed my vision as I saw Drake turn the corner and leave the corridor. Did he think I was like Ailla? I hoped not. But she'd thrown herself at him, too. And lied and lied to him, never caring that his feelings might be involved. Or that he might feel bad about the situation this put him in with his brother.

After all, like Ailla, I'd been raised by Eilor. For all Drake or anyone knew, it was the selfish upbringing of this Realm. I'd heard him rail about some of the abuses he'd found because Eilor was neglectful.

Did he see me in that manner? And while I thought he found me attractive, maybe that temporary lust was negated by who he thought I was? He seemed sincere when he spoke of being friends.

That must be it. He only wished to be friends and didn't want to be cruel. Even after being twisted and left for broken by Ailla, he was still the good, kind man he'd always been.

Oh, no. I went over my thoughts. I wasn't calling him pig-headed, or stubborn, or confounding, or any of the things I'd yelled at him in frustration since we'd come to the Dragon Realm. What was going on with me?

I put my hand on my door to steady myself. I felt dizzy, almost faint. I scrabbled for the handle, and nearly fell into my room when I opened the door.

I closed it behind me, feeling my face heat up at the closeness we'd just shared, and how stupid I'd been to misinterpret it.

He needed me to help him as he moved into governing the Dragon Realm. I wasn't a trusted figure, but I could tell that I wasn't the object of suspicion that I'd been, either. Drake, Taranath, and the rest of his family had seen to that. Just by allowing me to be with him.

I couldn't make that more than it was.

We were friends. Eventually, he would need to marry, to find a fae woman to create a family with. Someone to give him an heir.

I had a vision of Drake swinging a dark-haired little girl into the air, and I could hear the echoes of her squeals of laughter. His face was light, and his smile nearly broke my heart.

He deserved that. Deserved it all. And it wouldn't be with me. With a realization that was like being hit with a spell, I wanted that vision. I wanted that to be my daughter. I wanted to be the one who watched them indulgently, telling him not to get her all excited before bed, or dinner, or whatever it was we needed to go to.

How had this happened? How in the world had I fallen for Drake? For the Dragon King? I wasn't meant to be part of a court or a royal family...I'd only just gotten used to the idea of having something like a family that didn't involve me doing my utmost to avoid the other members.

I leaned against the door, almost faint with the awarebess of my feelings. I'd had no idea this was creeping up on me. I should have taken the time to think about why I didn't slap Drake when he'd kissed me earlier.

But I hadn't.

Would it have made any difference? It didn't hurt any less, the knowledge that I'd fallen—in love—with someone who was completely out of my reach.

The past month of working together, the fact that he was someone who considered me a friend, and even said so—I found that I cherished those moments.

And it didn't matter anymore.

Because I knew what would happen now. Now he'd be matched up. Some fae woman who would look at him as a catch now, versus before when he was a member of the Goblin King's court.

Would she be friends with him? Not if she was anything like the women who were Ailla's friends in the Dragon Court. He might even marry someone from this court, to solidify alliances or something equally boring and awful.

I made my way towards the bedchamber. All I wanted to do now was crawl into bed. I needed to make sure that I could put on a neutral face during the ceremony.

I'd try not to glare at all the eligible women. The ones who would be twittering and eyeing Drake.

He wasn't mine, and it wasn't my place to glare, or act in any way other than a friend and advisor to the king.

It also meant I would need to find a place for myself. Any wife who had any sense of being the queen of the castle, both in name and in meaning, wouldn't want a woman around who was a friend and close to her husband, even if he was the king.

Throwing myself onto my bed, I sighed. Just when I thought I might be finding my place, life showed me that it wasn't my place after all.

Maybe I could speak with Taranath. He might have some ideas. I sat up. That was a good idea. He wasn't a teller of tales, either. He'd keep my inquiries to himself. Maybe he could find a place for me in the Goblin Court?

I went to the mirror, looking to make sure that no traces of my distress showed. What was I thinking? I couldn't leave the Realm—I needed to care for the dragons. I didn't trust anyone else to do that. No one else had the ties to them that I did.

And no one other than Drake and Taranath had seen them. I couldn't leave. No matter how painful the new queen would be for me.

I decided that I'd go and see Taranath anyway.

Under the pretense of wanting to organize my place, and not wanting to bother Drake as he was preparing for his coronation.

I wiped at my face, even though I didn't think I'd been crying. And with grim determination, I went in search of Taranath.

There were a lot of people milling in the corridors. I could feel the energy from the bustle of activity leading up to the coronation. Not to mention, the death of Niles, and all the things Jharak had said. In fairness, it was a lot to take in. People wanted to talk.

A few made eye contact with me, two even tentatively smiling. Both young women, I noted. It was hard not to snarl because of course, they wanted to be friendly now that it was known I was part of the king's circle, right?

Instead, I nodded, keeping my nasty thoughts to myself. I sped up, not wanting to get caught in the conversation of any sort.

Finally, I reached the rooms where Taranath was staying. Close to where the other mages lived, and close to the workrooms. I knocked, hoping that he'd be within.

After a moment, Taranath himself answered the door.

"Lady Aine, to what do I owe the pleasure?" He inclined his head.

His formality made me choose my words more carefully than I might have. "I know that tonight is a busy night, but I was hoping to speak with you if it wouldn't take up too much of your time?"

His eyebrows went up, but he said, "Of course. If you'd care to come in?" He stepped away from the door.

I walked in, finding that I had a lot of nervous energy. I hoped that I would say the right thing, not embarrass myself or give myself away.

"How can I help you?" He walked in front of me, leading me towards a sitting area. It was amazing to watch him walk. He didn't look like he had feet under his robes. Taranath was the most graceful man I'd ever seen. Even more than—no. I wouldn't think about him in that way.

"I have been considering my future here in the Dragon Court," I began.

When Taranath gestured toward a chair, I sat, feeling restless, but not wanting to pace in front of him.

"When Drake is crowned, he will need to have a clear line of who are his advisors. Given my history here, I'm not sure I'm someone he wants to name publicly."

"Wouldn't this be a conversation for you to have with Lord Drake?" Taranath said gently.

"It will be," I said impatiently. "But I need advice on

how to sort this out before I speak with him. He'll have more than enough to manage without adding my concerns to the mix."

"Go on," Taranath said.

"I don't want to leave the Realm—I cannot. My concern is that as the royal family grows, a woman close to the king will not be..." I looked down at my hands, "Welcome. But," I looked up and heard my voice harden, "I cannot leave the dragons. There is no one else who can be trusted with them, nor do I believe that Fangorn would deal with anyone else."

A slight crease formed between Taranath's eyes. "I wasn't aware that Drake, once he is king, had any plans for anyone else to work as the liaison between the dragons," he said. "At least, not that I have heard."

I shrugged. "Things can change," I said. I wanted to say more but decided that discretion was probably a better choice.

Taranath didn't reply immediately. I got the sense he was choosing his words carefully. That was potentially alarming, as he always seemed to speak carefully.

"I don't believe that any...Woman chosen by Lord Drake will be anything other than..." he hesitated, looking at me, and then away. Then back at me. "Supportive of whatever path he chooses to take in regards to all matters in the Dragon Realm," he finished.

What in the name of the stars did that mean? That was a lot of words for no clear statement. I must have frowned because Taranath continued.

"After all the work you—we—have done to try and right the many wrongs in this Realm, you cannot think that he would take as a bride anyone not as committed. Not just committed to the Realm itself," he went on, "But committed to his vision for the Realm. You and I, Lady Aine, have been part of crafting that vision. Drake would be the first one to confirm that," he finished.

Then he peered at me. "What is it you are concerned with, my lady?"

"That as things...evolve, and change, there will be no place for me here. I'll be the strange women who were far too close to Eilor, the wretched king that everyone will claim to hate, and now, what exactly is it I am doing?" I got up, throwing up my hands in exasperation. "I didn't fit in before, and I am concerned that after things settle, I will find myself in the same place. Having seen a different sort of life through the eyes of Drake...and his family..." I added, "I don't want to be in such a place again." Now it was my turn to use a lot of words and not say anything.

How could I possibly tell him the truth?

Taranath covered his mouth with his hand and turned from me slightly. What did he know? What was so bad to create that sort of reaction? I started to speak, but my breath caught in my throat.

He didn't speak for a moment; then he took a deep breath.

Oh, no.

"Lady Aine, I honestly believe you are concerned for no reason. As far as I have heard, there has been no conversation about your role in this realm, outside of how you are paramount to unlocking coexisting with the dragons. I know that both the Fae King, as well as the Goblin King, in addition to Lord Drake, want to find a way to allow them to live differently than they have all these hundreds of years. You are critical to that. Not only because you are one of them, but because of how committed you are to caring for them. I think your fears for..." he looked at me, and pursed his lips, "The future is unfounded."

I stared. This was not what I'd expected to hear. "Do you believe that?"

Taranath nodded. "Of course I do. I wouldn't say so if I didn't believe it. I am surprised that this is a concern. You are a vital part of the rebirth of this realm, my lady, and to think otherwise devalues you in a way you do not deserve." He spoke forcefully.

This was what I wanted to hear. I would not be sent

away. No matter how painful it would be to see another woman at Drake's side, I would not be cast out.

I let out a sigh of breath.

"What has brought on this concern?" Taranath asked.

I shrugged. I couldn't tell him the truth, even though seeing him stare at me with those piercing eyes —Taranath had a way of asking questions that made you just want to answer him. I didn't think he used magic. From what I knew of him, he would consider it extraordinarily unethical. But his manner showed you that he truly cared, and that made me, at least, want to spill everything to him.

The problem was, he reported to Drake. And Brennan. And Jharak. I couldn't tell him the truth because he might feel he needed to tell one, or all of them. I couldn't deal with pity. I wouldn't. So I needed to keep my mouth shut on this matter.

But I needed to say *something*.

"I am looking to the future. When Drake is crowned, the dragons may very well be able to leave their cages. Matters will need to be addressed rapidly." I looked at him, hoping I sounded convincing enough. It was, after all, true. I was worried what would happen if the spell holding the cages shut was broken. We hadn't discussed what would happen if I went down to see them and they were awake and moving around freely. I didn't think that anyone had thought that far ahead.

It sounded plausible. Right?

Taranath narrowed his eyes at me, but I only stared back, daring him to go further.

He didn't.

"While that is a legitimate concern, I think that you can put your mind at ease. Anything decided about the dragons will include you. Since we are on that topic, what do you suggest should the coronation indeed free the dragons?"

"I think that as soon as the ceremony or whatever is supposed to happen happens, I need to go see them. Fangorn has no desire to create problems. The last time we spoke of it, he just wanted to be able to fly, and live freely."

"Do you believe him?"

I felt my temper flare, but I tamped it down. It was a fair question. "I do. Although he could probably tell me lies and I wouldn't know, I don't think he wants to fight or create problems. I think he wants to live out the rest of his life in peace and obscurity."

"Does he have a sense of the other ten?"

"He says all of them were against the war and were the most peaceful of the dragons. They may be angry, and I can't blame them. But I think that can be addressed without everything going to ruin," I added.

"What if they choose to leave? Will you go with them?"

I hadn't thought of that. "I don't know."

"I don't think it's something you need to decide now," Taranath said briskly. "And now, Lady Aine, if I have answered your questions adequately, I think you should retire. The next few days will be long for all of us."

I stared at him, but he'd already turned and was heading for the door to his rooms. I guess that was all I was going to get. At least he thought the idea of my leaving was not part of any discussion. That was a positive for me.

The rest of it, I would need to figure out on my own.

22

DRAKE

*H*e opened his eyes and took stock. It was morning. Today was—today was his coronation. He looked over at the table next to the bed. The dragon ring sat on it. With the blue stone turned to him, he felt almost as though it looked at him.

For the first time, however, he didn't feel like a fraud or an imposter.

After he'd talked with Aine, he'd taken a long time to return to his rooms. He'd avoided his family because he didn't want to deal with questions.

He'd not been able to avoid Taranath, who had knocked on his door, and asked if he could return the ring.

"Shouldn't you bring this to Jharak?" Drake asked.

"It's the ring of the Dragon King," Taranath said.

"We already know it responds...poorly to the Fae King. I feel it should be with you."

Drake hadn't been in the mood to argue.

Then Taranath spoke again. "If there is anything I can help you with, My lord, if you wish to talk or unburden yourself, I am at your service. I know that I am bound to the Goblin Court, and your brother, but you have my assurance that anything we may discuss will remain between us."

Even now, Drake had no idea what he was talking about. He'd thanked Taranath, and told him no. After a few moments, Taranath set the ring on the desk in the outer room and then left, silent as the night itself.

Drake wasn't sure what he'd missed, but he felt he'd missed something. Which didn't feel good.

But there was nothing to be done about it now. Today was all about presenting the right tone to the Realm. To all the Realms. Delegations from the Dwarf and Troll Realms would be arriving today. He made a mental note to ask Jharak if things had been smoothed over with the trolls. And to make sure that Iris stood far away from them. It would be poor form if Jharak had made nice and then the Goblin Queen offended them again because the smell made her ill. They were pungent; he thought with a grin as he threw his legs over the side of the bed. But he was used to goblins, so the trolls didn't create too much distress for him.

Trevan hurried in when he heard Drake get up. He'd been a good choice for a manservant, Drake thought.

"My lord! I am glad you've woken. We have a great deal to do today!" Trevan already sounded stressed.

"No need to make yourself upset," Drake said. "I will be as I always am, Drake. People can like it or not. So do your best, and don't worry. Anything unsightly will be all my fault," he grinned at the boy, who frowned.

"My lord, you're a handsome man, and well you should know it. Today is the day when you must look your best. I'll not have it otherwise!"

"I certainly won't get in your way," Drake said with a smile. "Have at it."

An hour later, he was ready to hit something. He'd never been one to fuss over how he looked, and Trevan apparently did nothing but.

Finally, Trevan declared himself satisfied. "You look every inch a king, my lord."

"It's all due to you, Trevan," Drake said with a smile. Thoughts of escape made him less annoyed.

"Now I need to go find my father, and we'll get this thing going," Drake added. He patted the pouch at his belt to make sure the ring was in it.

And he all but ran from the room before Trevan

could come at him with another comb or some other small thing that needed to be just so.

But once in the corridor, he slowed his run. He was the king or would be. His subjects needed to see him taking this seriously, and respecting the honor of the crown. Once he was king, he could be more of who he was, but it was important that people knew he would always do what was right.

He took side hallways to the rooms where his parents were. Entering quietly, he found Jharak looking out a window. He could hear Nerida speaking in another room, probably to her maidservant.

"Father?" He asked.

Jharak turned around, a smile lighting his face. "Drake, you look well."

"As well as I am going to," Drake muttered.

"Are you still sulking? It's a bit late for that," Jharak said.

Drake smiled. "No, not sulking. I merely remain surprised that I am to be a king. That's all. I expect it will take after a while."

Jharak laughed. "It will, although sometimes, you'll look around and wonder how you came to be here."

"I wonder that daily, Father, when yet another thing isn't working as it should," Drake said, thinking of all that had been done to make today possible.

"Once you have matters in hand, it will get easier," Jharak said.

"Your father is right," Nerida added, coming in and patting at her hair. "Drake, you look exactly as you should." She eyed him critically, and then nodded, apparently satisfied.

"How is that, Mother?" He asked.

"Like our son and a king," she said.

There were many things Drake could have said, but he chose none of them. Instead, he smiled at his mother, happy that their relationship had moved to a better place. It would take time for him to forgive all the things said. But this—things as he remembered them—this felt good.

"Thank you," Drake said. He smiled, and Nerida smiled in return. It was the first time Drake had seen a genuine smile from his mother since the existence of Cian was revealed when he'd left a shim blade and a note in the Goblin Castle threatening Brennan. How long ago that seemed.

"Well, don't you clean up nicely," Iris said behind them.

Drake turned. "I can say the same, ladyship," he bowed to her.

"Oh, shut it, your high and mightyness," Iris rolled her eyes as she rubbed her back. "How long do we think this whole shebang is going to take?"

"It's not every day a new king is crowned," Nerida began.

"The ceremony will not take too long," Jharak interjected. "But all of the court will swear fealty to the new king, and that may take some time. I have made sure there is a chair for you, my dear," he smiled at Iris.

"Thank god," she said. "I wouldn't make it."

Nerida made a noise that sounded a great deal like a huff, but she didn't say anything. Drake thought that was probably wise.

A knock at the door brought Taranath in, along with Brennan.

"Everything is ready," Taranath said.

Drake wasn't sure who he was addressing.

"Is the staff holding up?" Drake asked.

Taranath nodded. "There is a great deal of excitement, my lord. That, and talk of the coming market. I hope you don't mind that I've permitted them to watch the events of today before the celebration."

"Of course not," Drake said.

"They can't be any worse than the goblins," Brennan added.

"I miss them," Drake admitted.

"They miss you, too," Iris said. "I'm not sure why, but they do. They're also very proud of you. Like you're a beloved son or something."

Drake smiled. "It's a shame you know nothing about such a distinction," he said smugly to Iris.

"You can think that if you like," she shot back.

"I think they dote on her even more than they dote on me," Brennan said, smiling at his wife.

"Well, an heir gets everyone all emotional," Drake said.

"Your turn is coming, dragon boy," Iris said.

Her comment had the effect of a cold chill through the room. Drake noted that everyone stopped what they were doing, and turned to look at him.

"What are you talking about?" He said, to break the ice that had just formed.

"Brennan and I are doing our part for the team," Iris continued. "Now you need to do yours. You need to look around, and—" she stopped as Brennan coughed.

"And what?" Drake asked. Aine came to mind at that moment. What he wanted was to—what he wanted wasn't possible. She didn't care for him the way he'd come to care for her. He needed to quit thinking about her, or anything like Iris was suggesting.

"And see who might be an appropriate partner," Iris finished.

Drake noted, out of the corner of his eye, that both Brennan and Nerida were giving Iris the 'be quiet' look.

Almost as if they'd been—"Have you been

discussing this matter in my absence?" Drake asked.

"Yes," Iris said before anyone else could speak. "One of the ways to make sure that you have a stable footing is to take a wife and begin to create a family. A new royal family for the Dragon Court. No one wants to say anything because apparently, you're so fragile, it might get you all upset," she waved a hand in the air. "But I know better, and beating around the bush is not the way to approach this."

"Oh? And do you have someone in mind?" Drake asked. He couldn't keep the frost from his tone.

Iris ignored him. "I do, but—"

Whatever she was going to say was cut off by Aine's entering the room.

Drake turned to greet her, and his mouth fell open.

Aine wore a blueish green dress that flowed around her. As she came into the room, he could see that there were jewels or some decoration on the dress that made it sparkle as she walked. Her hair was up and decorated with the same sparkly jewels, or whatever they were. Her lips had been darkened, and it made her eyes look more intense against her fair skin.

"I knew that would look good on you!" Iris exclaimed, walking to Aine. "You look fantastic!"

"Thank you," Aine said, almost shyly. "Thank you for the help you sent along with the dress."

"That was my pleasure," Nerida said, smiling.

Drake didn't realize that his mother even really knew of Aine, much less liked her enough to send someone to help her dress.

Then he wondered why he hadn't thought of such a thing. It was, after all, his castle.

He had the answer without asking. Aine didn't ask for help. She didn't ask for anything. She managed.

Just like he did.

A pang hit him when he considered how similar, how well matched they were.

Why didn't she care for him?

Could he woo her? Show her that he was a good choice? They would be good together if she could only see it.

"Aine, I am happy to assign you someone to look after you," he said, hoping he didn't sound pompous or foolish. "I'll take care of it after everything today."

Aine smiled. "Thank you, that will be nice. I did want to ask if there was time for me to go and see Fangorn. I would like to talk to him before the actual ceremony."

"The Lady Aine and I spent some time discussing what might happen with the dragons after the reign of Eilor is broken," Taranath said. "We are unsure if the cages will open, or what might happen. I think it's wise to speak with Fangorn to coordinate in case he and his fellow dragons find themselves free."

"Dragons running loose in the castle might create some problems," Brennan said with a smile.

"By all means, go and speak with him. We have time, yes?" Drake looked at his father. After all, it wasn't him who was running things. This was all Jharak.

Jharak nodded. "You have about an hour, Aine. Give our regards to Fangorn, and let him know that I am willing to speak with him whenever he wishes. Or not at all, if that is his wish."

Aine smiled at him. "I appreciate your concern. I know that Grandfather will as well. I think, in speaking with both of you, that you are both very different from the people you were when the dragon war ended."

"That's my hope," Jharak said. "You should go so that you have time. We'll meet you back in the hall."

Aine nodded, and looked around, her eyes meeting Drake's last. "I'll be there. I just need to see him today," she added.

Drake felt like she was speaking to him alone.

He nodded, wondering when he'd be able to move on from how he felt for her.

She wouldn't be leaving his court. So...never?

He kept himself from sighing, and instead said, "Of course."

Aine looked around at everyone again and then hurried from the room.

It felt like everyone watched her leave. She looked stunning. Drake couldn't blame them.

"Thank you," he said to Iris and Nerida. "I'm ashamed I didn't think of it before but thank you for providing her what was needed."

Drake couldn't understand why they both smiled at him in the same manner.

"Of course," Nerida said. Then she shared a glance with Iris, who smiled.

What was going on here?

Thankfully, Jharak interrupted this—whatever this was, saying, "Drake, let's go over how things are going to proceed."

He was able to put the thoughts of the strange behavior of his family and Aine from his mind. Because no matter their nagging, he would not take a wife unless he loved her. And he loved Aine. If she would not have him, he would need to wait until he stopped loving her, or found some kind of love with another.

Which meant he would have to resign himself to being alone. He couldn't imagine loving another as he loved Aine. He couldn't tell when it had happened, or how, but it had.

No one else would do. So it was better that he distract himself from thoughts of her.

For the moment.

23

AINE

I sped away from the guest chambers, my heart thumping in my chest. I'd been so nervous about this dress, the hair, all the things that Iris had sent for me. Along with the maid that Nerida sent to help me dress.

I wasn't used to it. I stroked the fabric of the dress. I could get used to it, however. This was lovely, and the admiration I'd seen in the eyes of everyone in that room back there—especially Drake's—made it even better.

The coronation had to go well. Without a problem, or anyone popping in to claim the throne, or cause a problem, or try to kill him.

I hurried to the corridor and flew through the door. Then down the stairway, and I burst into the cavern.

The lights all flared, and Fangorn came to the front of his cage.

"Daughter, you are stunning."

He was in fae form today, and I reached for his hands through the bars.

"Thank you. I wanted to see you before the ceremony. If things go as we hope—" I stopped, afraid that if I spoke, I would ruin any chance of good fortune.

"Things will happen as they will," Fangorn squeezed my hands.

"If the doors should open, I must ask that you manage everyone down here," I said. "It will go poorly if you all are free and things go badly."

"Do not fear, Aine. I will keep the last of us safe."

I heard the resolve in his voice.

"Thank you. I'm worried," I confessed.

"I know, and I appreciate it on our behalf. But in this, trust me. And convey my assurances to your king."

I looked up, and he smiled at me. "I will," I said.

"Aine," he began, his voice softer.

"What?" I wasn't sure I wanted to hear what he was going to say. I couldn't read his thoughts, but I had a sense.

"I think you need to be honest with your king as well."

My head dropped so that he wouldn't see the

sudden tears that rushed to my eyes. "I...I have tried. It was not a successful attempt."

Fangorn didn't respond. When I finally had the courage to look up, he had an expression of disbelief on his face.

"I think you might be mistaken, daughter," he said.

I shook my head. "I don't think so." I was so sad about the manner in which my attempts with Drake had been received; I didn't have the strength to deny like I usually did.

"Well, perhaps give it time, and try for honesty again," Fangorn tipped my head up so that I was forced to look at him. "You might be surprised."

"I'll be back down after the ceremony," I said, pulling away. I didn't want to talk about Drake anymore.

"You make me proud," he said as I turned away.

At his words, I flashed a smile at him, and then I hurried back. I hated that I left him alone once more. Hopefully, that would not be the case much longer.

I was almost running as I passed Drake's quarters on the way to the hall. Midway there, I caught up with Drake and his family.

"My lady," Taranath said quietly.

Drake's head snapped around. "That was faster than I expected," he said to me, beckoning me to join him. "Is all well?"

I knew he didn't want to mention the dragons out here where others might hear.

"Yes. I went over what should happen if doors open," I said. I glanced around, but no one outside of the family was nearby. "He said to let you know that he will not allow anything to happen that would be problematic." Well, that is basically what he said.

Drake nodded. "Good. After the court does all their swearing, bowing and scraping, you can go and see what happened."

I smiled, and it felt genuine. "That was my thought as well."

"It's good that we are of similar mind," Drake smiled at me, almost as if he were trying to tell me something.

I hadn't realized that we stopped, staring at one another until Iris cleared her throat behind us. "We do need to go a bit further," she said, her brows raised.

"Easy, your ladyship," Drake grinned at her. "You'll be stuck in the hall soon enough."

That made Iris laugh, and her laugh was so lovely, all of the staff and courtiers that were in the corridor stopped and stared. After a moment, I could see that the people around us were smiling.

"This is a good way to start a new reign," Jharak murmured. "Let's go get this started, shall we?"

He moved around all of us, leading Nerida with

him. "Brennan, you and Iris follow. Then Aine and Taranath, and finally, Drake will be announced."

His calm manner spurred everyone into motion again, people lining up as he had requested.

Taranath held out an arm, and I rested my hand on it. As Jharak approached the door to the hall, I saw that Trevan, Drake's servant, hovered around the doors. He leaped to attention when he saw us.

The doors flew open, and Trevan nodded to one of the guards who'd opened them.

I walked in with Taranath, barely hearing my name announced, or much of anything. I felt the weight of the eyes of the entire Court on me, and it felt almost stifling.

The entire ceremony felt that way, except when Jharak had Drake kneel, and then placed a crown—I didn't even know this Realm had a crown—on Drake's head and the dragon ring on his finger. Drake rose, and the sun shone into the hall.

He faced the court and recited his pledge to them and the Realm. I could feel tears prick my eyes at how strong he sounded.

Jharak had not only provided a chair for Iris, but for everyone who stood with Drake. It was a good thing, as the fealty offerings of the courtiers took a long time. I ignored the simpering of some of the younger women of the Court.

I also ignored Iris patting my hand. I kept my smile pasted on.

Once the ceremony ended Drake invited everyone into the dining hall, which was adjacent to the great hall. He turned around to face the rest of us.

"Well, it's done." He looked tired.

"May I?" I asked.

He nodded. "But do not tarry. You will need to sit with all of us. We can't have you disappearing." Again, he smiled at me in that quiet, meaningful way.

I curtsied low, glad to see that we were back on some kind of even footing. "Of course not, your majesty. I shall do my best to hurry."

I left the hall, hoping to see that the dragons—my family—were now free.

24

DRAKE

*D*rake woke with the sun and stretched. What a busy two days it had been. The celebrations lasted until the previous evening. Finally, he called a halt, feigning old age. His court had laughed, and gradually, people made their way home, or to bed. Somewhere other than his dining hall.

His parents and brother had left this morning. Drake felt that he needed to crawl back into bed and sleep for another two days.

For him, the festivities had been marred by the fact that the dragons were still not free. The thought that Eilor might be alive was like a buzzing insect that he couldn't swat away. He'd mentioned it to his father and Brennan; they agreed to meet about it when the festivities were done. Jharak seemed to think if—and it was a big if—Eilor was alive, he'd lay low. Which would give them time to prepare.

He deliberately ignored thoughts of Eilor. No need to think on him any further just yet.

Perhaps he could go back to sleep for a while. Take a day to be lazy. Then he sighed, and got out of bed. As the king, that would never work. He would enjoy the peace he had now—

The door burst open. No knocking.

Aine.

"Yes?" He asked.

She raced in, her face alight. He'd not seen her much, and he knew that she was trying to keep a low profile, to let him take the center of attention. He also knew she'd been visiting the dragons. Her sadness weighed heavily on her.

Until now.

"It's happened!" She beamed at him.

"What?" He'd not seen her this excited in...Well, ever.

"The cages! I went down this morning, and Fangorn had opened his cage. The rest are unlocked as well! They are free!" Her joy radiated from her.

He felt a bit more uneasy. Free dragons were not going to be a problem easily solved. He'd been sending down live sheep, but what to do with them was a lot more difficult than just mustering up fresh meat.

"That's good, then?" He asked.

She nodded. "Yes. Fangorn believes that Eilor is truly dead. With you as the king, and his cage open, there is no way the man is alive."

"Good. I didn't want to admit it, but his surety makes me feel better." A weight lifted off him, more like it.

"Well then," she said. "I must go. I just wanted you to—"

Drake was out of his chair, and he took her hand before she fled from him once more.

"Aine, we must talk."

Her head dropped, and he couldn't see her face.

"No—"

"Yes. I have been thinking about what happened between us. I was going to apologize, but I no longer feel the need to do so."

Her head snapped up.

"Why not?" She sounded fierce.

"Because I have another solution."

"And that is?"

"I want you by my side. You love this Realm, even with all its problems. And I..." he took a breath. "I love you. It's been happening so gradually that I didn't realize until I did. Will you stand with me, help me to rebuild this? Together, we can solve even the fact that far too many dragons are living in the bottom of our castle." He lifted her chin so that he could see her eyes. He hoped with all the hope he had that he hadn't overstepped with her.

As they met his, Aine's eyes glowed a bright, intense green. Like her grandfather's.

"Yes," she whispered.

"As my wife?" he asked softly.

"Yes, Drake," she whispered.

He crushed her to him.

When their lips met, he thought he could never be happier.

Even if he would have to admit that his family was right.

But it didn't matter.

He wasn't alone, not anymore.

The End

A NOTE FROM LISA MANIFOLD

The End of The Realm?

While this completes the stories that I started in HEART OF THE GOBLIN KING, this is by no means the end. If you've been reading The Aumahnee Prophecy series I am writing with Corinne O'Flynn, you'll see that there are some familiar faces in that series as well. I love the Realm, and I love the fae world that I've created. My fae are amazing, and I can't just retire them, LOL. How far they've come since Brennan and Drake landed on Iris in a bathroom.

The next part of The Realm series are the last four short stories. They will end with EILOR'S TALE, and that will move everything along to my new series, The

Dragon Thief. No release date on that yet, but it's this year.

Thank you for all the emails, and the conversation, and the questions. This book came from you, my readers. I love y'all for that. I love this story, but it wasn't part of the original outline. Now I can rest easy, because Drake isn't left alone and miserable, and neither is Aine.

So no, The Realm is not ending. If anything, it keeps expanding.

Lisa

ALSO BY LISA MANIFOLD

The Sisters of the Curse Series

Thea's Tale

One Night at the Ball

Casimir's Journey

Heart of the Djinn Series

Three Wishes

Forgotten Wishes (2017)

Hidden Wishes (2017)

The Realm Series

Heart of the Goblin King

To Wed the Goblin King

Realms of the Goblin King

Rise of the Dragon King

The Realm Companion Tales, Vol. 1

The Realm Companion Tales, Vol. 2 (2017)

The Aumahnee Prophecy Series

with Corinne O'Flynn

The Portal Keepers *(Short Story)*

The Gimcrackers *(Short Story)*

Marigold's Tale *(Series Prequel)*

Eamonn's Tale *(Series Prequel)*

Watchers of the Veil *(Book One)*

For more information about this series and the related worlds, please visit The Aumahnee World

ABOUT THE AUTHOR

Lisa Manifold is a USA Today bestselling author of the series The Realm, Sisters of the Curse, Heart of the Djinn, The Aumahnee Prophecy, and coming in late 2017, The Dragon Thief. She writes paranormal romance and urban fantasy. She currently serves on the board of Rocky Mountain Fiction Writers as the IPAL Liaison, representing the indie authors in the organization. In 2016, she was honored as the RMFW Independent Writer of the Year.

Lisa lives in the great state of Colorado, with no

plans to live anywhere else. She is a fan of all things Con, and in fact, has a room at home dedicated to all the costumes. Lisa is usually running late because "Just one more page!"

She lives with her husband, sons, and three wonderful, demanding, rescue dogs. Adoption is the best!

You can find her on Facebook, Twitter, Amazon, or at www.lisamanifold.com. To keep up with all her newest releases, and various shenanigans, please sign up for her Newsletter!

Stay connected...

www.lisamanifold.com

lisa@lisamanifold.com